AF598844

RYOHGO NARITA

ILLUSTRATION BY
KATSUMI ENAMI

Report on Firo Prochainezo

A: Firo Prochainezo.

The thing about him is, he's far too "normal" relative to the other subjects of this investigation.

Of course, his immortality is plenty unique, but if you ignore that, his only distinguishing feature is his baby face.

While he is a gangster, he's quite down-to-earth... compared to the rest anyway. I doubt we'll need to worry much about him. As a matter of fact, he may be fairly easy to manipulate when we need to deal with the other dangerous characters.

Mr. Prochainezo holds his boss, Molsa Martillo, as well as one of the top executives, Maiza Avaro, in high regard. That's a weakness. He also seems quite infatuated with his roommate, Ennis. He's got all sorts of vulnerabilities we could exploit.

B: I'm against touching those.
While they are indeed vulnerabilities, they may also be, to borrow an Asian proverb, the lone scale that makes a dragon fly into a rage when it is touched.
No matter how peculiar the circumstances, Firo Prochainezo made it out of Alcatraz Federal Penitentiary with his freedom. Furthermore, he may have Szilard Quates's knowledge at his behest.
He certainly isn't an opponent we can afford to be careless with. Please stay on your guard.

Report on Ladd Russo

A: Speaking of men who are back from Alcatraz, the one we should really watch ourselves around is Ladd Russo.

He made it out by cutting sundry deals, but he's a murderer. It's strange that he hasn't been executed already. He's extremely dangerous, and if he sets his sights on us, we'll have a hard time stopping him.

Like Firo, he's got a woman in his life. Lua seems to actively wish for her own death, though. There's no telling whether she'll work as a hostage.

I think we should handle this one with the greatest possible caution.

B: I agree we should be careful, but I have a few things to note. It's true that Ladd Russo is a fearsome murderer, but his targets are exclusively people who think in a certain way, which makes it possible to predict his actions and avoid his attacks.

The unpredictable one is Ladd's underling, a young man named Graham Specter. The things he says and does are utterly incoherent. He doesn't do the killing, but we should assume his actions are always determined by a sort of mental roulette.

And, as unstable as he is, people say his physical abilities are even greater than Ladd Russo's... The world really isn't fair, is it?

On top of that, Graham is popular with quite a lot of people, including Jacuzzi Splot, the leader of a gang of delinquents, and someone named Shaft. It's impossible to understand.

Report on Victor Talbot

A: It was surprisingly easy to collect information on Victor Talbot. Apparently, he doesn't feel the need to hide.

However, the organization he belongs to has multiple advantages: an extraordinarily sturdy wall of information and extremely long feelers for intelligence. If we're careless enough to make a move on them, they're likely to uncover our weaknesses instead, and that would put our entire operation in danger.

That said, I have less faith in the intelligence of Victor himself.

B: He may be dim, but he's competent. I believe we should assume he's successfully using his wits to compensate for his stupidity.

A: So you don't deny that he's an idiot?

B: No, I'm entirely in agreement with you there.

Report on ???
A: The man who's next to Ladd Russo...? No, I saw the materials, but I don't think he's anyone Mr. Runorata needs to be concerned about.
B: I concur. There's nothing particularly noteworthy about him. No doubt he's simply one of Ladd's hangers-on, like that Who fellow.

Design: Yoshihiko Kamabe

VOLUME 18

RYOHGO NARITA
ILLUSTRATION BY **KATSUMI ENAMI**

NEW YORK

BACCANO!, Volume 18: 1935-A DEEP MARBLE
RYOHGO NARITA

Translation by Taylor Engel
Cover art by Katsumi Enami

Yen On
150 West 30th Street, 19th Floor
New York, NY 10001

Visit us at yenpress.com
facebook.com/yenpress
twitter.com/yenpress
yenpress.tumblr.com
instagram.com/yenpress

First Yen On Edition: January 2022

Yen On is an imprint of Yen Press, LLC.
The Yen On name and logo are trademarks of Yen Press, LLC.

Library of Congress Cataloging-in-Publication Data
Names: Narita, Ryōgo, 1980- author. | Engel, Taylor, translator.
Title: Baccano! / Ryohgo Narita ; translation by Taylor Engel.
Description: First Yen On edition. | New York : Yen On, 2016-
Identifiers: LCCN 2015045300 | ISBN 9780316270366 (v. 1 : hardback) | ISBN 9780316270397 (v. 2 : hardback) | ISBN 9780316270410 (v. 3 : hardback) | ISBN 9780316270434 (v. 4 : hardback) | ISBN 9780316558662 (v. 5 : hardback) | ISBN 9780316442275 (v. 6 : hardback) | ISBN 9780316442312 (v. 7 : hardback) | ISBN 9780316442329 (v. 8 : hardback) | ISBN 9780316442343 (v. 9 : hardback) | ISBN 9780316442367 (v. 10 : hardback) | ISBN 9781975356859 (v. 11 : hardback) | ISBN 9781975384715 (v. 12 : hardback) | ISBN 9781975384739 (v. 13 : hardback) | ISBN 9781975384753 (v. 14 : hardback) | ISBN 9781975384777 (v. 15 : hardback) | ISBN 9781975321567 (v. 16 : hardback) | ISBN 9781975321901 (v. 17 : hardback) | ISBN 9781975321925 (v. 18 : hardback)
Subjects: CYAC: Science fiction. | Nineteen twenties—Fiction. | Organized crime—Fiction. | Prohibition—Fiction. | BISAC: FICTION / Science Fiction / Adventure.
Classification: LCC PZ7.1.N37 Bac 2016 | DDC [Fic]—dc23
LC record available at http://lccn.loc.gov/2015045300

ISBNs: 978-1-9753-2192-5 (hardcover)
978-1-9753-2193-2 (ebook)

1 3 5 7 9 10 8 6 4 2

LSC-C

Printed in the United States of America

When I grow up, I'm gonna be a hero!
Yeah, like Wyatt Earp or Jesse James!
Just you watch—I'll get super strong!
And then, hey... I could protect you, too, if you want.

Oh, wow!
That's amazing! You're so keen,   !
If it's you, I'm sure you'll get really, really strong,   !
That's a promise,   !

Prelude

Step up. It's time to gamble.

Bets look fair, but they're not.

They're rigged to favor those with money and brains.

On top of that, ultimately, they're set up so the house wins. That's just how it is.

Don't go talking about good and bad luck. Anyone with genuinely good luck doesn't need gambling to be flush.

Others were born with bad luck and a mind to match— They're the ones who've got plenty of cash but gamble for the thrill of it, or maybe they just want to ruin themselves.

That aside, now it's your turn to gamble, despite your bad luck.

So what will you bet?

Money? Your life? Your pride? Your family? Your pals? Your sweetheart?

Choose carefully, more carefully than when you pick your roulette number.

The game's already started.

After all, the question of what you'll use for your chip is another bet.

I'll say it again: Choose carefully.

Even if you nail your number on the roulette wheel, it won't change how you put someone or something precious to you on the edge of a cliff for your own convenience.

Once you've made something a chip, you'll treat it more casually—way more than you think you will. It'll be easier to bet the second time. By the third time, you'll actually start thinking, *I don't care if I lose. I don't care if they take this from me.*

That's true no matter how weighty a conviction it is. Even if it's your entire fortune, or your family, or your life.

Come on, it's time to gamble. This is the moment of destiny.

What will you put on the table?

You already gambled away your chance at a decent life to a sticky-fingered demon—so tell me your stakes, Mr. Immortal.

Digression The Prologue Doesn't Exist

A certain month in 2003 In a corner somewhere

Rosetta, hmm?

I'm not sure whether I should rejoice at our reunion or introduce myself for the first time.

Perhaps any greeting would be meaningless.

Well, never mind.

It doesn't matter whether this encounter is a coincidence or an inevitability that you wished for.

However, if you'd like to make small talk, I will keep you company.

⇔

The 1935 incident?

Yes. Of course I remember it.

It was a difficult affair to forget… Although, it seems you weren't able to be a part of the fray yourself. Perhaps you should consider yourself fortunate.

But this is why I expect you've seen only a part of it.

There's regret in your expression.

No matter what you think now, we made our choice.

In order to leave the bottle, we had to sacrifice perfection.

I chose the world, and you chose the future.

That said, those imperfections allow us to enjoy this world well enough. Don't they?

Well, never mind.

If you're bored, you may enjoy events in places beyond the scope of your power, on television or in the papers.

Personally, I entertain myself with unpredictable futures and others' creations.

After all, even if you read the creator's mind, there's no guarantee the finished work will reflect it.

Yes, that's right. I remember every detail of that incident back in 1935.

No doubt a bygone world you never knew will seem like fiction to you, Rosetta.

What? How did that incident begin in the first place? ...Now, that's an interesting question.

It had no clear "beginning." Therefore, if that incident were a story, one could say there would be no prologue.

If one did exist, it would be the events that had occurred earlier...

The commotion surrounding the liquor of immortality, for example, during which Firo and his family became immortal. Perhaps the incident on the Flying Pussyfoot, or the uproar at Mist Wall. The events in Alcatraz and Chicago would qualify as well.

We could go still further back, when Maiza and the others encountered me onboard the ship...

Back to when you and I were born...

Taken to extremes, perhaps one could say the prologue was the beginning of the world itself.

That wasn't a joke.

As a matter of fact, the 1935 incident occurred because a variety of pasts became entangled with one another.

* * *

Do you understand now that this incident has nothing resembling a beginning? However, if I had to say… Hmm. Let's assume that, as a columnist for a gossip paper, I wrote a column about that incident. In that case, I should begin by relating the disaster that befell Firo.

Why Firo, you ask?

Hmm. True, misfortunes and incidents happened to others during the same period.

An extraordinary number of people were involved in that incident, after all—many of whom were at the center of one event but in the dark regarding others.

I'm beginning with Firo simply because the story is easier to tell that way.

There was a little reporter named Carol—well, I suppose now, she's a renowned journalist whose name has gone down in history, but in any case—back when she was a rookie, she once described him to Gustav as "main character-ish." What a fascinating perspective she has. No wonder she's carved out success for herself.

I imagine she meant that he possessed a sort of charisma. She's right; he does have something splendid that draws people to him. It's different from what Isaac and Miria possess.

Hmm? …Do you know those two, Rosetta? If you don't, I'll explain later.

Ah. You don't know much about Firo to begin with, do you? This is becoming quite a chore.

…Oh. Yes, I'm probably partial to him because he's part of my circle, but…as the Martillo Family secretary, I think highly of Firo.

This is true even from my position as a so-called demon.

Don't look at me like that. Although I do understand why you'd doubt me.

I taught him his knife-fighting, after all.

If I show him a little favoritism, just indulge me.

Chapter 1 The Youngest Brother Isn't in High Spirits

"Say, listen, Isaac!"

"What is it, Miria?!"

One afternoon, when glimpses of blue sky peeked between the New York skyscrapers, an easygoing couple was having a conversation on the streets.

"You know what? I just realized something amazing!"

"Did you?! You really are incredible, Miria! I didn't realize anything at all!"

People who didn't know them thought, *What's with those two dimwits?* and eyed them suspiciously as they passed. However, locals who frequently saw them walked past with weak smiles, thinking, *There they go again.*

Among them, there were a few who murmured, "I haven't seen them in quite a while..." Of course they hadn't. Up until very recently, the man had been in prison.

Be that as it may, if those people had heard Isaac had been in the famous Alcatraz Federal Penitentiary, most of them—especially those who knew the pair pretty well—would have laughed it off: *Applesauce!*

Alcatraz was an escape-proof prison, which housed only the most dangerous of America's criminals. Anyone could have told you this man didn't belong there.

Not only that, but there was no way he could have gotten out again in just a few months, much less been capable of lighthearted conversation afterward.

However, despite their doubts, the truth couldn't be twisted.

The man of this couple had definitely been to Alcatraz.

Isaac Dian and Miria Harvent were outlaws who'd committed a series of strange robberies and thefts all over the United States. These extraordinary troublemakers had stolen things ranging from chocolate to a very wealthy man's legacy, leaving their ultimate goal so unclear that all the agents chasing them had been confounded.

They had turned over a new leaf and were now living ordinary lives.

Isaac, who'd been cleared of all charges through a special plea bargain, was relishing his freedom with Miria, whom the law had overlooked.

"So what is this amazing thing, Miria?"

"Well! You see, Isaac! We've run out of money, you know?"

The fact he was free meant, in essence, that he was unemployed.

"Ha-ha-ha! I see, yes, that is amazing! ...Huh?!" Isaac turned to look at Miria with round, flustered eyes. This was a normal reaction, but Isaac being Isaac, what he was worried about was a little different from what would have worried most people.

"Old Yaguruma said not having money was the same as not having a head! H-hey, Miria! Are we going to lose our heads?!"

"Yes, Sleepy Hollow! The Headless Horseman!"

"The Legend of Sleepy Hollow" was a folktale about a headless cavalry soldier, which had been told in New York since the colonial era. The writer Washington Irving had turned it into a short story, causing the tale to spread rapidly. At this point, it was one of the east coast's most famous legends.

"D-don't tell me... If we don't have money, will the Headless Horseman come and cut our heads off?!"

"I'm scared! Wh-what'll we do, Isaac?!"

"Come to think of it, I heard something else from Old Yaguruma: Even Satan in hell is motivated by money... Does that mean if we can't slip a bribe to Satan, we'll lose our heads?! ...Wait, have we talked about this before?"

"That means this conversation's important enough to have several times, Isaac!"

As a matter of fact, every time their assets had hit rock bottom, they'd had a similar conversation just before stealing money from the mafia or some other mob outfit. They had since retired from robbery, though, so neither of them even suggested trying that now.

"Hmm... Work, eh? What should we do for work, Miria?"

"Um... I think we just have to earn money, Isaac!"

They had practically no experience with legally sanctioned employment. Isaac had worked while he was an inmate in Alcatraz, but that was about it. They'd prospected for gold a few years ago, but they'd thought of it as "stealing treasure from the Earth," so they didn't consider it a job. Plus, no one had hired them, so even the people around them had just assumed they were digging a dried-up mining gallery for fun.

"I see... We'll do work and draw wages for it... Should we be bankers, maybe?"

"Yes, the money game! Monopoly!"

"What are you supposed to do at banks, though? I can't run financial calculations." Isaac had only a vague understanding of the job.

"Maybe it's about getting rid of bank robbers, Isaac."

"Oh, I see! That's great, Miria! After all, we know a whole lot about robbery! I'm pretty sure there's an Eastern proverb that goes... erm... 'If you know your enemy, and you know everything about yourself, then yesterday's enemy is today's friend'!"

"Yes, no sides! Friendly fire!"

The remarks accomplished nothing but to boost their own moods as the pair headed briskly for a nearby bank...

And after they had been tossed out of every bank in an average of thirty seconds, they went to a nearby park, sat on the grass, and talked.

"Hmm. All the banks told us they weren't hiring at this time."

"Yes, we must have picked the wrong time to come."

"I guess time really is money."

"Yes, the time thieves won this round..."

The two sighed dejectedly. "We have to work."

A few passersby who knew them overheard and also heaved weary sighs. *These two seem happy all year round, and even* they're *looking glum. Times really are hard*, they thought.

It had been a couple years since the National Prohibition Act was abolished nationwide.

The Great Depression, which had begun on Wall Street in 1929, had left deep wounds on America and all around the world. Perhaps it was still clawing away at the global economy and people's everyday lives. Many people were out of work, and more and more individuals with nowhere to go were getting involved in shady businesses.

Underworld organizations had also taken a hit from the Depression, but by attacking the incompetence of the government, they could get the common people on their side. It certainly did seem as if the claws of the recession were mixing up the public and hidden sides of society.

In 1933, a turning point came.

President Franklin D. Roosevelt, who'd taken office that March, fought the beast using every method at his disposal, from frontal breakthroughs to indirect attacks.

After he took office, the government temporarily closed all the banks and conducted a thorough internal inspection. One could have termed it a declaration of war on the Depression from the United States of America.

And so, the long fight against the invisible beast began:

The abolition of the Prohibition Act.

The abolition of the gold standard and a transition to a planned monetary system.

The beginning of the public works project that built dams in the Tennessee River Valley.

Job training for the unemployed, conducted by the Civilian Conservation Corps, which was known as "the CCC."

On top of that, armed with the program commonly referred to as the New Deal—which included some policies that skated very close to the line and were later judged to be unconstitutional—America plunged into battle against the looming recession.

In the late spring of 1935, a large-scale public work promotion agency known as the Works Progress Administration would be established, creating jobs for several million unemployed workers.

But it was February now, and most of those several million people were unemployed at this time.

The monster of the Depression was still on the prowl, and America stood its ground against it. The fight would continue until the onset of a global turning point: World War II.

The struggle was currently at its climax; it was a conflict of historic proportions, one that would determine whether or not the sun rose for the citizens who were struggling in the darkness.

That was how things stood in 1935.

Still, even in the midst of that era, some rootless wanderers drifted where the wind took them and took no notice of the ongoing crisis. This pair remained optimistic, indifferent to the whole situation.

"Okay, Miria, that settles it! Let's look for work!"

"Yes, it's a journey in search of work! The start of an adventure!"

"For now, we'll go around visiting everyone we know and ask them if they've got a job for us. Friends really are a great thing to have, aren't they, Miria?!"

"Yes, yesterday's friend is a friend today, and tomorrow, and every day after!"

What results would their optimism bring?

No one knew.

Not yet anyway.

⇔

Same day, night   Somewhere in New York   An underground casino

It was a magnificent space.

Las Vegas wouldn't be transformed into an earthly paradise glowing with neon signs for another decade or two.

In this era, when an unprecedented recession was surging through America and the policies of the New Deal had begun to show people a glimmer of hope, gambling was heavily regulated in most states.

Granted, that wouldn't change even after the dawn of the twenty-first century, but the visitors to this extraordinary realm had no way of knowing that.

Their eyes lit up as they set foot inside, and not only due to the magnificent interior; it was more a reaction to the territory they were about to venture into. Essentially, they were excited to gamble.

The guilty pleasure of doing something illegal, the thrill of wavering between destruction and success, would stir fevered emotions in any heart.

This was a casino. A place of gambling, created by gambling, for the purpose of gambling. No other words were necessary.

Here, "gambling" was the motto and an absolute presence.

Winners and losers were made here, and sometimes entire lives were reset. This place was isolated from the world outside; luck could turn justice on its head.

And since it was a casino, size didn't matter.

This was a small underground casino in a corner of New York. Naturally, it was illegal and unauthorized, and its clientele were hardly refined—although, every so often, customers who seemed wealthy stopped in as well. The relatively narrow room was enveloped in an indescribable chaos.

Within that room was a young man who seemed terribly bored.

Firo Prochainezo had a boyish face, but he was past twenty already.

Although most people his age still wouldn't be trusted with much, he'd risen to a distinguished rank in the Martillo Family, an illegal syndicate. He was also the person in charge of this underground casino. However, a certain complicated "characteristic" of his kept widening the gap between his age and his looks, to the point where people who didn't know him mistook him for a boy who was wandering around the casino playing scofflaw.

That said, if they planned to earn a little extra dough because of that impression, they'd lose more than just their money.

As Firo leaned against the wall in a corner of the casino, even the regulars who knew him well were eyeing him.

The reason was simple: It was the first time he'd been there in a full two and a half months.

While he was gone, a certain whispered rumor had traveled through the community of regulars:

"I heard Firo Prochainezo got charged by the DOI."

Assuming the casino might be in chaos since the young guy who ran it wasn't there, those visitors had been by daily, thinking this might be their chance to win.

Ironically, this meant the casino had pulled in record earnings due to its manager's absence, and Firo couldn't hide the fact that he was sore about it.

The regulars, however, failed to notice this as they kept shooting him complicated looks. "We heard they'd put him under glass, so how come he got back this fast?" they whispered.

As a faint, prickly tension began to run through the glittering space, a man spoke to Firo, apparently unaffected.

"Are congratulations of some sort in order?"

He seemed to be about the same age as Firo, but the piercing air around him suggested that he was more of an underworld veteran than Firo was. Luck Gandor was the youngest of the three brothers who ran the Gandor Family, a mafia group with territory nearby.

"Oh, Luck. I didn't see you come in… Congratulations for what?"

"For making it back from Alcatraz in one piece, or for the fact that the Martillo Family didn't hold you accountable for the incident. Either is fine."

At his childhood friend's remark, Firo sighed. "Man, your ears are as sharp as ever."

"We're a small outfit. If we didn't have sharp ears, we wouldn't survive."

"Well, either way, I don't need congratulations for all that. It'll just make everything feel worse." Shrugging, Firo surveyed the casino again.

The place was fitted out with the classic gaming facilities: baccarat and blackjack tables and roulette wheels, surrounded by clusters of gamblers with superficial calm and extremely intense eyes. A row of slot machines stood against the wall opposite Firo and Luck, and multiple people were taking turns at them, their eyes darting around in dismay.

"Would you look at that. They're Liberty Bells." Noticing that the slot machines were different from the type that was currently nearing the height of its popularity, Luck gazed at them, intrigued.

Pleased that he'd stolen a march on his knowledgeable friend, Firo cheered up and started telling him about the machines with some pride. "They're not on the market yet. Apparently, they're practically prototypes. Ronny brought them in from somewhere."

"To celebrate your release?"

"All right, all right, knock it off." Sighing again, Firo took a step forward. "From what I hear, they've got some sort of original musical instrument inside them. When you win, the thing makes a hell of a racket, but it sounds nice. It's so good that when the jackpot signal plays, everyone in the place starts clapping."

Slowly, Firo cut across the casino.

Luck followed him, listening to what he was saying—but as they walked, he picked up on something.

Firo's attention wasn't on him. It was focused elsewhere.

"When the other fellas see that, they want people to clap for them, too, so they shove their money into the machine, and the winners want that kick again, so they let the slots hoover up their winnings."

"I see." Realizing what his friend was about to do, Luck took care to act natural as he responded.

That was when Firo turned back to Luck—and grabbed the hand of a man who'd been out of his line of sight, behind a blackjack table.

"Gyagh!"

Firo twisted the man's arm behind him, and cards fell out of his sleeve. "We can't have that, sir. We don't let our guests bring their own cards." While Firo did take a polite tone, he also brought his weight down on that twisted arm. "You used the same trick three years back, didn't you? I remember banning you. Don't tell me you thought this would be water under the bridge by now..."

The grifter's eyes were tearing up as he overcame the pain to shout, "Shove off! Th-this place is a clip joint anyway! At mafia casinos, in the back, they—eh...eh, oh...kuh...buh."

The man's shriek trailed off in the middle, and he slowly passed out, foaming from his mouth and nose.

"We're not mafia. We're Camorra."

Luck saw that during the exchange, one of Firo's hands had circled the man's throat; he'd shoved his thumb in deep, crushing his Adam's apple. Imagining the pain, Luck unconsciously rubbed his own throat.

As they watched the scene play out, the customers gulped, and time in the casino stopped.

Once you threw a wet blanket on their fun or shut down their lucky roll, the guests might be jolted out of their fantasies and leave the casino.

That was what Luck thought, but Firo was used to dealing with situations like this. Letting go of the man, he clapped his hands together and spoke in a cheerful voice. "Sorry to disturb you, folks! As an apology, I'll give you all a round of Alveare's special honey liquor on the house, so please keep enjoying yourselves."

Signaling for his staff to take the fallen cheater away, the casino manager smiled breezily.

"If anybody lost money to the magician here, speak up within the next five minutes. We'll check his wallet, and I guarantee we'll return as much of your money as possible!" he joked.

It wasn't a terribly witty joke, but it had broken the tension, and about half the customers started to chuckle.

Luck was impressed; the way Firo had called out to his customers sounded nothing like the way he normally talked. Firo turned toward him again, falling back into his usual voice.

"Sorry about the noise, Luck." After he'd made sure that things had calmed down in the casino, Firo headed for the office in the back.

As Luck followed him, he gave a wry smile and spoke in a low voice: "...It feels as though I see the same thing every time I come here."

"That's because there are lots of morons who see we're not a big outfit and sell us short. They figure we can't call the cops if they bull their way through, and they'll probably manage to make a clean get-away from a smaller syndicate."

Once the pair entered a different room and closed the door behind them, Luck asked a question that was only half-serious. "So you're not actually cheating?"

"You know we don't have to. It's set up so the house wins even if we don't do a thing."

As a matter of fact, there weren't many Americans who assumed that the house cheated at underground casinos. No one would go near an illegal gambling den that was rumored to clip its patrons; they'd take their business to a place with a fairer image.

At Firo's casino, they used dice made of crystal or glass, and it was possible to place roulette bets even after the ball was launched.

"Well, if someone's winning too much, I do recommend they try their luck at cards." Firo's face clouded over. "Although, I did that to Isaac a while ago, and the dealer completely screwed up. We ended up dropping a bundle, dammit." With a weary shake of his head, Firo went on griping about his friend. "After all, Prohibition's over. Alveare ain't a speako anymore. It's doing well out in the open, but the casino still attracts the same dangerous crowd as ever."

Not that Firo had a problem with the situation. He continued, even smiling in mild self-mockery. "New Jersey allowed casinos five years back, but New York isn't even considering doing the same. What's up with that anyway?"

"But that's perfect, isn't it? The fact that it's not legal is precisely why you're rich, Firo." Brushing away his friend's complaint with a little smile, Luck admonished him lightly. "Or are you saying you're confident you don't need shady tactics to beat casinos built by the giants of Wall Street or the rich men of Millionaires' Row?"

Firo thought that over. "...Well, nah, not that confident." He could maneuver during turf wars; there was no way he could compete fairly in business. Then, to camouflage his discomfort, he steered the conversation off topic. "Either way, we're illegal, which means that bastard Edward could bust in here at any minute, which means I don't have time to let my guard down. Of course, I'm here because I want to be, so I've got no complaints, but still."

"Edward, hmm...? I hear he's a rather well-known member of the Division of Investigation."

"A DOI agent who's well-known ain't worth squat."

Firo reached for the office cupboard, intending to have a drink. He didn't have a snack to go with it, but gossip about the absent lawman would do.

However, when Luck asked his next question, his eyes looked rather serious. "Getting down to business: What happened over these past two months?"

"...What, weren't you here to celebrate my getting out?"

"I meant to, and I wasn't planning to ask any questions, but you seem a little odd."

"I do, huh?"

Firo played dumb, and Luck continued. "Ordinarily, you would have handled that card sharp simply by signaling your men with a glance. But you hurt him personally... You're strangely on edge—almost as if you're on the lookout for something."

"......"

Firo was silent.

Luck went on anyway. "If it's a personal matter, then I'm an outsider, and I should just let you be. But I'm in charge of an organization that operates nearby. If there's a situation that could end up affecting us, I need to set aside our relationship as sworn brothers and learn what I can."

"...You're as much of a boss as ever."

"As I said, precisely because we're small, we can't afford to let our ears and noses lose their edge." Luck grinned, but his eyes remained sharp.

Firo sighed, giving up. Then, bit by bit, he began to tell him. "All right. Hear me out and don't get mad. I don't really know what's about to happen, either. I just think something's gonna. That part's for sure."

"What do you mean?"

"I'd better give you a rundown of what happened during those two months."

To Luck's eyes, his friend still seemed evasive despite what he was saying.

"Uh..." Firo paused. "First, cut me some slack—there are some parts I don't completely get, and I'm skipping the stuff that's personally embarrassing. The situation should still make sense anyway."

"Yes, that's fine."

"Well, let's see... Where should I start? ...Yeah, probably when that jerk Edward took me in, and there was this asshole immortal in the interrogation room."

Immortal.

The moment he heard that word, Luck straightened up, focusing more intently.

It wasn't that he'd been listening casually before. He'd been planning to pay close attention, as the boss of a mafia outfit. Now that the word *immortal* had come up, though, he had to be wary for additional reasons.

After all, both Firo Prochainezo and Luck Gandor were immortals themselves, people with a unique and rare characteristic.

On top of that, there was one other thing that worried Luck. If this involved immortals, he'd have to consider the possibility that the Runorata Family, one of the area's leading syndicates, would come into it, even if they seemed unrelated at first glance.

"I see. Making the trip to someone else's turf just paid off." Luck leaned against the wall of the office, automatically scanning his surroundings.

Firo also checked to make sure there was no one else in the office, then focused part of his attention on the casino, visible through the window.

Lowering his voice a bit, he began to tell the story.

* * *

But then, he saw a man coming down the stairs on the opposite side of the casino, the ones that led up to its ground-level entrance.

Breaking off for a moment, Firo gave the man a once-over.

That fella hasn't been here before.

Due to the nature of this place, Firo was automatically wary of new faces.

Of course, since the casino wasn't completely invitation-only, there were plenty of newcomers. Firo considered it his responsibility as the manager to be at least a little wary of all of them.

That said, due to the timing, he was a bit warier than usual at the moment.

The man wasn't doing anything particularly suspicious, though, so Firo decided to keep half an eye on him through the office window while he resumed his conversation with Luck.

There was something Firo didn't know: This man, a completely new face to him, was a puzzle piece from the incident that surrounded Firo and the other immortals. More accurately, he'd been involved for a few years now.

His name was—

Chapter 2 No Rest for the Agents

A few days earlier Somewhere in New York Victor's investigation headquarters

"Don't you dare tell me you don't know. Shut the hell up."

In a storehouse in one of the brand-new warehouse districts on the outskirts of Manhattan, a simple row of desks had been set up and covered with messy piles of transmitters and documents.

In this extremely sparse investigation headquarters, a man with glasses spoke in a loud, irritated voice. "How many weeks has it been since Huey evaporated from his goddamned cell at the end of the year? Are you people incompetent? Damn right you are! And so am I. We haven't found one damn clue about what that terrorist is up to!"

The man, whose temples were twitching as he berated both his subordinates and himself, was Victor Talbot. One of his men, Bill, scratched at his own temple and drawled, "Uh... Well, I understand that you're upset with Laforet, but would you go on, Assistant Director?"

"...Yeah, you're right. Sorry 'bout that."

Apologizing with surprising meekness, Victor—assistant director of a special department that existed within the Division of Investigation—took another look around the warehouse. Bill and Donald, who'd been working under him for a while now, were in there; he also spotted Edward Noah, who'd acquired too much dignity for them to get away with calling him "newbie" at this point.

The Bureau of Investigation had undergone a name change in 1933, becoming the Division of Investigation, but the positions Victor and his men held were still the same. He'd heard a rumor that the name would change again in July, this time to the Federal Bureau of Investigation, but his group's distinctive character probably wouldn't even flicker.

Around the men who'd been with him for long years were several unfamiliar faces. Their eyes were focused either on Victor or on their sheaves of documents. Everyone looked tense. They were new members—agents who'd been brought in as reinforcements when the terrorist Huey Laforet had broken out of jail.

They were dealing with immortals, beings that shattered preconceived notions, so naturally, they'd been strictly screened to ensure their philosophies and personalities would be a good fit.

However, that wasn't the only problem.

"Just to be on the safe side, I'm gonna ask—how much do the newbies understand?" Victor asked.

"Uh… What do you mean by 'understand,' sir?" Bill replied.

"Okay, here's a question: You over there, new kid. Who's our enemy?"

The person he'd abruptly called on responded without a moment's hesitation. "Those who would harm the nation."

"Tch… Correct," Victor grumbled.

Edward was familiar with the man's personality by now and understood the meaning behind his boss's frustration. *He probably wanted the newbie to say "It's Huey Laforet" so he could show off and tell him, "Absolutely wrong, you idiot!"* Edward heaved a mental sigh over his boss, who was in the habit of acting overly controlling in weird situations.

Oblivious to his subordinate's feelings, Victor impassively went on with his lecture.

"Not everyone who's involved with the elixir of immortality is the enemy. Whether they're immortals or demons, we'll pull the ones we can use over to our side and make 'em work for the good of the country… Although it's pointless to hope for hard work from a bunch who can just exist forever."

It's often said that people live in order to die. Victor had predicted that when people who'd gained eternal life got lazy and started to think, *I'll get around to it someday*, their *someday* would never come, so they'd grow lazier.

And in fact, once they'd lost their mortal time limit, several of the immortals he knew had degraded into apathetic ennui before they eventually disappeared.

Of course, they hadn't vanished of their own accord. They'd all been consumed by the hand of a guy named Szilard Quates.

Immortals.

As the word implied, they had escaped the irreversible current that flowed from life to death, gaining the right to live forever.

Thanks to the alchemical elixir of immortality, they had acquired bodies that would never age. In addition, those bodies would regenerate completely from any disaster whatsoever, even if they were cut into tiny pieces, burned, ground to a paste, or dissolved in acid.

According to the demon who'd given Victor and the others the elixir, there was only one way for them to die. He'd said it was a measure for when they grew tired of living, when eternity was nothing but despair for them.

Fellow immortals were able to kill one another.

Or more accurately, they could absorb the other into themselves. To use one turn of phrase, eat them.

They'd place their right hand on the other's head and focus on their wish to eat.

With nothing more than that simple *magic word*, the immortals—who could survive a dip in molten lava or a beheading—would summarily vanish from this world.

All the knowledge they'd stored up over those long years would be inherited by the one who'd eaten them.

Assuming the newcomers would already know this about the immortals, Victor went on. "Even if the likes of terrorists and the mafia weren't interested in eternal life, they'd probably be real keen on the idea of pawns that won't go down. You fellas need to keep a sharp lookout for those antisocial elements and for spies from enemy nations… Especially spies. For example, if they made somebody who held classified intel drink the elixir of immortality, then ate them…all those secrets would be theirs."

"In that case, you mean an actual immortal would be working as a spy?"

"That's right. Don't try to size up immortals using common sense. Not only do they not die, they've lived several hundred years. They're like storybook vampires; you've gotta take a different idea of common sense than you're used to. *Particularly* when it comes to the ones that didn't get lazy."

Remembering Huey's face, Victor ground his teeth as he went on. "You've already pounded the name Szilard Quates into your heads, right? The old guy was greedy as hell. He was the type who wanted money, power, everything. He also wanted knowledge twice as much as the next guy. Lots of alchemists have an unlimited thirst for knowledge. That means some of 'em would eat their comrades just because they want to know precisely what they know."

When they heard those words, although the newbies nodded gravely, one doubt seemed to have occurred to them. Donald noticed that they seemed hesitant to put it into words, so he spoke up in their place. "You look like you're wondering whether our Assistant Director is that type."

Bill picked up where he'd left off. "Uh… Well, can't say as I'm surprised. The assistant director does seem pretty possessive."

Victor clammed up, temples twitching.

The newbies looked away, trying not to meet his eyes.

"…Don't worry, kids. You'll just have to take my word for it: As a scholar by nature, I do have a thirst for knowledge. Unlike Szilard, though, there's no knowledge I want so bad I'd eat some other guy's brain to get it." Managing to swallow his irritation, although it took some doing, Victor clicked his tongue. "I hate other people's leftovers, see?" He returned his gaze to the documents. "Immortality? The ability to eat other people? You can get to the truth without that stuff."

This didn't seem much like a lecture for new recruits, but the agents who'd been recently assigned to this department were listening to him seriously. They'd probably already sensed the truth for themselves, somehow. Immortals weren't a fairy tale, a delusion, or some sort of camouflage. They actually existed.

"Were those suits you're wearing made by immortals? What about the shoes on your feet? The guns on your hips? Have you heard any rumors that the designer at Colt's Manufacturing Company was an immortal?"

"Erm… Sorry to butt in, but Donald and I have Smith and Wessons," Bill said.

"Don't interrupt," Victor shot back, a vein on his forehead threatening to burst. Then he took his gun from its holster and set it on the desk. "Listen up: You can't kill an immortal with a gun, but you can stop 'em in their tracks. If you plug them in the head, they'll be unconscious until they regenerate. However, enemies that ain't immortal—mafia, terrorists, those fellas—will die if you put a bullet through their skulls. In exchange, assume they're a whole lot more used to shoot-outs than we are."

He stared at the handgun on the desk. His voice was clear throughout the room. "The greatest weapon we've got isn't a gun. It's the fact that we're fighting for the country. America will endorse you in the pursuit of justice. If you do your jobs right, I will, too. Assume you'll be able to support the country just as much as other agents. Before too long, you won't have to buy your own guns; they'll be issued to you."

Adding irrelevant remarks as he went, Victor continued. "Well, we shouldn't have any fellas here who've been corrupted by mafia bribes, but…I'll be praying that you men stay on the side of justice.

"I won't stop you from getting greedy and becoming immortals. Just be real careful not to become enemies of the state."

⇔

Ten minutes later

After their "class" had ended, Victor and the rest of the group got to work summarizing the current situation.

Using chalk, he wrote on a blackboard, which had been nailed to the wall of the warehouse.

"All right. Lemme give you the lowdown on the garbage dump you're gonna be watching."

The first letters he wrote spelled out *The Martillo Family.*

"So first off, don't take your eyes off these guys. They're mafia—they call themselves Camorra, but a gang of criminals by any other name is just as rotten. They're a small outfit whose turf covers parts of Little Italy and Chinatown. They're not worth paying attention to."

He snorted, but then his expression abruptly turned serious.

"...Except for the fact that some of their execs are immortals."

He tacked several photos to a corkboard that hung beside the chalkboard, the first one being an elderly man.

"This guy's the boss, Molsa Martillo. I hear he came over from Naples, but it doesn't sound like he made any substantial contact with immortals while he was there. That said..."

Victor turned to the next photo he'd tacked up, which showed a bespectacled young man. Victor resettled his own glasses on his nose.

"This one's Maiza Avaro. He's also from Italy—specifically Lotto Valentino, which is over by Naples—and there's a good possibility that's why he and Molsa hit it off."

Lotto Valentino.

Maiza Avaro.

When those two names came up, a ripple of tension ran through the newbies. They'd seen both of them mentioned here and there in the materials they'd been given ahead of time, often enough to leave an impression. Once the new agents actually read through the materials in detail, they came to the conclusion Maiza Avaro and Lotto Valentino were the origin point of everything they had to deal with.

At this point, Lotto Valentino was a simple tourist spot, but it had once been a city of research that had attracted alchemists from all over Europe. Maiza had apparently been the oldest son of one of the town's noblemen, but he'd studied alchemy and had left the area. No one knew how it had happened. Along with many other alchemists who'd assembled in Lotto Valentino, he'd boarded a ship bound for America, the *Advena Avis.*

Huey Laforet, who would go on to become a terrorist, and Victor Talbot, who would join the Bureau of Investigation, had both been on that ship. They'd been members of the group that had formed around Maiza.

In that sense, the man with whom Victor had the most fateful connection was Maiza.

"We don't have a complete handle on whether or not Maiza spread the knowledge of immortality around. However, even if we don't know all the details, it's a fact that he got his hands on Szilard Quates's elixir of immortality. And Szilard, the guy who'd made the elixir..."

At that point, Victor tacked up a new photo.

It showed a baby-faced young man in a pale green suit. He appeared to be somewhere in his mid to late teens.

"He got eaten by this fella, one Firo Prochainezo."

"How did that kid end up immortal? Did Maiza give him that stuff to drink?"

It was a perfectly natural question, and Victor shrugged, shaking his head. "No clue. Even I dunno the details there. I don't even know how many other members of the Martillos drank it. What's important ain't how he got that liquor. It's what he's planning to do now... Well, we did get him to work for us once, but that doesn't mean we can slack off on watching him."

The next photo he pinned to the board showed a woman with rather short brown hair who was wearing a man's suit. "So this doll here is Firo's servant. She was originally an actual doll—a homunculus—created by old Szilard, but there's a note about that in your materials, so I'll skip the explanation. The important thing is that she's got knowledge of all sorts of martial arts stored in that brain of hers. If you assume she's a frail woman, she'll break your neck for you, so watch it."

That could have been either a joke or a serious warning. Victor tacked up photos of the executives one after another, elaborating as he went. He pinned materials—including photos taken without the subjects' knowledge—to the corkboard, covering everything from major executives like Ronny Schiatto and Kanshichirou Yaguruma to Pezzo and Randy, who were relatively low-ranking members.

He was clearly proud that there was nothing the Division of Investigation couldn't find out.

However, a voice echoed through the warehouse, easily destroying that mood.

"I see. Very well researched."

The voice seemed to have come from the upper reaches of the warehouse. Every agent in the room looked up, but all they saw was a perfectly ordinary ceiling. There didn't seem to be anything wrong with it. Bewildered, the agents let their eyes return to the front of the room, and that's when they saw him.

"Granted, it's all superficial, but you've done a meticulous job here. Quite admirable," the man commented quietly.

He was standing in front of the corkboard, scrutinizing the materials that were tacked to it.

"Waourwagh?!"

The strange yelp had come from Victor, who was closest to the man.

Up until just a moment ago, no one had been nearby, and yet an unfamiliar man had abruptly appeared right in front of him. You really couldn't blame Victor for his less-than-cool reaction.

"Wh-why, you…!"

"Relax. I'm unarmed. If you're foolish enough to start a gunfight here, you'll only gun each other down. I'd hate to be the cause of that, but… Well, never mind."

Seeing several of the men reach for the roscoes at their hips, the man spoke calmly.

At that point, the agents realized something.

They'd seen this man's face a few minutes earlier, in a photograph on the corkboard.

"Ronny...Schiatto." Victor's voice was a strangled groan.

Removing his hat, Ronny spoke dispassionately. "Hmm. I thought I'd leave you to it, but I have one correction to make. Look at the twelfth line on page three of our *caposocietà*'s personal history. You have his name as 'Malsa Martillo.' You should watch your spelling. If there were an actual person named Malsa Martillo, you'd have the makings of a false charge here."

What the man said sounded like a joke, but for some reason, no one felt like disobeying him. In spite of themselves, the trainees turned to the relevant page and promptly found the spelling error there. The fact that a man who had just appeared had pointed this out meant the materials had been leaked, and the tension in the warehouse ratcheted up a notch.

What should they do with this guy?

Taking positions that would let them draw their weapons at any moment, the agents focused their attention on their on-site commander.

The commander—Victor—held up a hand. "Calm down, men. Unless he makes a move, don't touch your guns." Then, giving the other man an appraising look, he quickly grimaced. "I remember now... You're the magician who threatened me last year, huh."

About two months ago, after he'd made Firo Prochainezo his pawn and sent him to Alcatraz, Victor had paid the Martillo Family a visit. Things had gotten ugly, and after Kanshichirou Yaguruma had tossed him across the room, this strange man had shown him something peculiar. Victor had explained it away as sleight of hand, but even if the guy was a fellow resident of New York City, he couldn't explain away the fact that he'd turned up right here, right now, as a conjuring trick.

Even as he held back his subordinates, Victor gave the man an openly hostile glare.

Ronny's expression clouded over slightly, and he sighed. "You even had a photo, and you didn't realize it until just now...? Is my face that forgettable?"

Ronny was genuinely concerned, but to Victor, the remark sounded like a taunt. Even so, he responded with sarcasm, not anger.

"Yeah, well, you were the hardest one to find dirt on. There's all sorts of stuff about you in connection to the Martillos, but your past is a total blank. You know what? Enough of this. I'll get it out of you at my leisure, after I arrest you for unlawful entry."

"That would be a problem. Telling you about my past in depth would take several years at the least. If you'll compensate my company for the damages my absence will cause them, I could take it under consideration, but..."

Victor knew Ronny had said *company* because, at present, the Martillo Family was publicly posing as a company that operated restaurants. They'd probably managed to break into the business, even in the middle of the recession, by making skillful use of connections from their speakeasy days.

"You think you've got the right to refuse?"

Victor's response was only natural. Ronny put a hand to his chin, thinking. "When exactly did I enter illegally?"

"Huh? What kind of bull...?" Just as he was about to say *bullshit*, it happened.

Out of nowhere, wind blew inside the warehouse, scattering the materials stacked on the desk into the air.

The paper acted as a smoke screen, blocking the agents' view, but only for a moment.

In the next instant, their vision cleared, and they saw Ronny Schiatto standing outside the window, in the street that ran behind the warehouse.

"...Huh?" Victor sputtered.

Bill and Donald had stayed calm, but Edward's eyes were wide with surprise, and the newbies couldn't even seem to get their questions straight in their minds.

At some point, Ronny had relocated to a spot outside the window.

That was plenty strange enough all on its own, but there was something else.

"Um... I, uh... Was there *always* a window there?"

Bill's question froze all the newbies' spines at once.

However, the incomprehensible situation actually calmed Victor down. He fired a question through the window, his eyes sharp. "What the hell did you do?"

"Why don't we agree to call it...magic?" Ronny's face was expressionless as he made this proposal, and Victor found himself at a loss for words.

Without waiting for his answer, the man who was the Martillo Family's *chiamatore*, or secretary, spoke to the new agents. "Well, never mind. Rookies, this is the world you've stepped into."

Strangely, although Ronny was speaking from the other side of a closed window, his voice echoed clearly all throughout the warehouse.

It was almost as if he was speaking directly into their minds.

"I'm not sure whether I should welcome you to this side of things, or *deal with* you here... Well, never mind."

⟺

Two minutes later

After Ronny Schiatto made himself scarce, the investigation headquarters recovered from its confusion.

They'd covered the window with a spare corkboard, and all the scattered documents had been collected.

Part of the reason they'd managed to calm down a mere hundred and twenty seconds after seeing something that bizarre was the fact that they were outstanding agents. The rest was probably because they had already spent so much time recognizing that they were dealing with immortality, something beyond the bounds of common sense.

Victor was impressed, but he wasn't about to show it. "You've still got a ways to go. Kids, you gotta learn how to calm down in five seconds. When you get to my level, a magic trick like that won't even shake you up in the first place."

Once he was finished bluffing, he resumed his lecture. The first photo he posted showed a small child.

"Czeslaw Meyer. He's an immortal who came over to America on the ship with me. God knows why, but he's staying with the Martillo Family, too. He's also suspicious, in various ways."

He took Czes's photo over to the blackboard and stuck it up with cellophane tape. Cellophane tape had been invented only five years ago, but the radical discovery had spread around the world, radiating a sense of prosperity in the midst of the Great Depression.

"Right, right. Even this cellophane tape wasn't the work of an immortal. Humans made this. You don't need to be afraid of magicians like our recent trespasser, or of this Czeslaw kid, either, obviously."

When Victor, a former alchemist, had first seen cellophane tape, he'd said, "Why didn't I come up with this stuff?" He'd been thoroughly frustrated, but as if to say he'd already forgotten about that, he put the tape to work.

Although the incident a little while earlier had made the rookie agents freeze up, this positive side of his was gradually helping them relax.

That is, until they saw the two photos Victor stuck to the board next; their hearts skipped again.

"Prior to a few years ago, this kid apparently had a connection to this guy. It wasn't direct, but we know he made contact with a group who had the guy's personal support for a few things."

One of the photos showed an old, bespectacled man: Bartolo Runorata. No one needed to be told he was the head of the Runorata Family, one of the five biggest syndicates on the east coast.

"And then, behind the scenes, Bartolo here is linked to this guy… Although it may have nothing to do with the immortals."

The other photo showed a late-middle-aged man with a distinctive mild smile: Cal Muybridge. He was also famous enough that he needed no introduction. He was a giant who was the founder and current chairman of Nebula, a Chicago conglomerate.

"On top of that, when we checked into the connection between Bartolo and Nebula specifically with regard to the immortals, one other name came up."

He smacked another photo onto the board, exasperated. Its subject was Manfred Beriam. He was a senator, and the fact that a photo of him had turned up here sent a new current of tension through the rookies.

Nodding in apparent satisfaction at their response, Victor tapped the photo of Czes on the blackboard.

"Check that out: All we did was poke this one immortal who looks like a little kid, and look how big it's gotten. Now do you see just what kind of battlefield this department is standing in the middle of?"

The newbies' silence was as good as agreement.

Victor went on.

"There's no telling what the hell this innocent-looking kid might be plotting at this very moment."

⟺

Meanwhile New York, somewhere in Little Italy The restaurant Alveare

"So what are you cooking up this time, Czes?"

"Let us in on it."

In the bar, an abnormally thin man and a fat man were talking to a boy.

The boy, Czeslaw Meyer—who only appeared to be around ten years old—grinned at them.

"Um, next, I'm thinking of hiding Firo's clothes while he's in the shower. Then, while he's trying to find them, I'll have Ennis take him another set."

Czes's scheme made the men in the place cackle loudly.

"That's rich! He'll turn red as beet, fling the window open, and jump right out!"

"Nah, he won't be thinkin' that hard. He'll dive straight through the glass, count on it."

The boy was planning a dumb prank on his naïve companion, and the executives of a criminal organization were getting in on the action.

In the middle of this extremely peaceful scene, a man poked his head in through the restaurant's door.

"Huh? Hello, Mr. Ronny. Where did you go?" Czes immediately switched his attitude from mischievous to well-mannered.

As Ronny answered, his face stayed expressionless. "Mm… There was an error in some paperwork. I corrected it."

"It's pretty rare for you to make a mistake, Mr. Ronny."

"No, the mistake wasn't mine… Well, never mind. Everyone errs sometimes." Sitting down at the counter beside the table where Czes and the others were, Ronny muttered to himself. "I'd like to go without another error for a little while, at least."

"What are you talking about?" Czes cocked his head, perplexed.

Gently dropping his left hand onto the kid's head, Ronny smiled faintly. Then he said something that, to Czes, sounded like nothing more than a joke.

"Even I can't rewind time, you see. I'm just hoping no one dies."

⇔

Meanwhile   Somewhere in New York   Victor's investigation headquarters

After a glance at the silent rookies, Victor got back to the main topic again.

He stuck another photo below Bartolo's.

There was a handwritten name on the photo: *Begg Garrott.*

"This guy's Begg. He's an immortal and Bartolo's protégé of sorts, but at this point, he's just a petty thug who pushes dope. Sure, he's an enemy of the state, but he ain't the type to come up with massive plans… That said, don't get careless around him."

As he listened, Edward thought, *The one who seems most likely to get careless is Victor,* but he didn't say it. Compensating for their boss's flaws was one of their jobs. He focused on the information that was accumulating on the boards.

The posted intel outlined a "current situation" that was split across several groups.

1) Huey Laforet

He was the core of the meeting's topic and the root cause of the whole affair.

Huey Laforet was an immortal who used a variety of terrorist units—the Lemures, Larva, Rhythm, Time, Sham, Hilton—as his pawns for acts of terror all over the country.

Until just the other day, he'd been in Alcatraz Federal Penitentiary, locked away in a special cell not shown on any map. However, he'd successfully broken out through Hilton's special power and his unique characteristics as an immortal, and his whereabouts were currently unknown. After one last reported sighting in Chicago, he'd managed to completely disappear.

Huey possessed special information networks known as Sham and Hilton. Based on what the division had heard from Firo, who'd infiltrated Alcatraz for them, Victor and his associates had determined that it would be extraordinarily difficult to shut those networks down. That meant they'd need to accept that a certain amount of their intel would be leaked to their opponent and find a way to outfox them.

2) The Martillo Family

The group's importance had been explained in detail earlier.

There had been a change in the last few minutes, though; Ronny Schiatto's photo had acquired the word *Dangerous*, inked on in bold letters.

3) The Gandor Family

This New York mafia outfit, which interacted with the Martillo Family, was rumored to have been involved in several immortal-related incidents. More than anything, the underworld rumor that the Gandor bosses were immortal was being treated as important information the division couldn't afford to ignore.

Three brothers—Keith, Berga, and Luck—ran the organization as its top executives. They were an odd group. Their turf was small, but they stayed independent, and they hadn't put themselves under the protection of one of the big syndicates.

There had also been sightings of a saloon girl wielding two Japanese swords and of a guy who constantly walked around with scissors. There was definitely something about them that set them apart from ordinary mafia groups.

4) The Runorata Family

In addition to their connections with Czeslaw and Begg, they'd caused trouble with the Gandor Family in the past, and the DOI was looking into them from a variety of angles. There was a rumor the Runoratas were keeping an enormous bear on their property, too. The outfit was a hotbed of potential trouble.

In terms of violence alone, they were one of the strongest organizations linked to the immortals, and the division would probably have to cooperate with other departments in order to gather information on them.

Nonetheless, Victor's policy was that, if their course of action overlapped with that of another department, their own department should prioritize actions related to the immortals.

5) The Nebula conglomerate

Founded by Cal Muybridge, Nebula had initially been a small company that planned events and manufactured equipment for amusement parks. However, it had grown into a global corporation with a truly diversified administration. It was involved in everything from grocery sales and chemical engineering to ironworking and insurance, and lately it had branched out into publishing and weapons development.

Earlier in the year, an incident involving the immortals had occurred at Mist Wall in New York—and although Victor's group had had a hard time believing it, it appeared as though more than a thousand employees had been turned into incomplete immortals: people who would regenerate from injuries but continue to age.

In addition, the corporation was connected to the Lemures' 1931 occupation of the Flying Pussyfoot; Nebula had owned the train on which the incident occurred.

On top of that, they were believed to have been deeply involved in the Chicago affair two months ago, and a focused investigation that targeted them was currently underway.

6) Senator Manfred Beriam

As one of the most influential members of the Senate, he had both financial clout and political might, plus hand-trained private soldiers. Victor had received information that Beriam had employed a man named Spike, who had originally been one of Huey Laforet's subordinates, and he might have had connections to Huey.

If that information was true, it would mean that Beriam *had picked up one of the terrorists who'd once taken his wife and daughter hostage*, which meant he was more than worth keeping an eye on.

Due to Beriam's position, the division had to move carefully.

He was on friendly terms with Nebula, and he'd made use of his political position to hush up the Flying Pussyfoot incident.

7) A gang of delinquents in New York

There was a group of juvenile delinquents who were led by a young man named Jacuzzi Splot.

At a glance, they didn't seem to have any connection to the immortals. However, they'd been spotted during the incident in Chicago that had been discussed earlier, the Mist Wall incident, and also the 1931 incident on the Flying Pussyfoot, which meant they were definitely people of interest. For reasons unknown, they'd become caretakers of the Genoard family's second residence on Millionaires' Row and were using it as their base.

Their relationship with the affluent Genoard family was currently under investigation.

8) The Russo Family

A syndicate in Chicago believed to have had ties to Nebula.

Their boss, Placido Russo, was missing, and the syndicate was effectively wiped out.

Placido's son and daughter-in-law were already dead, and his grandchild Ricardo Russo was missing as well. Apparently, all the young thugs he'd trained had vanished from Chicago.

There was one other concerned party whose family name was Russo.

"Does this Ladd Russo goon want to take over the syndicate?" Victor asked.

Bill scratched his temple. "Hmm... I really couldn't tell you. It's true he's a pretty dangerous character, but..."

Ladd Russo was Placido's nephew and allegedly a hitman employed by the Russo Family. The division hadn't been able to prosecute him for murder due to lack of evidence, but he'd been sent to Alcatraz for his assault on the Flying Pussyfoot in 1931.

That said, since that entire incident had been covered up, the fact of the matter was that they'd scraped together other crimes and somehow managed to put him away.

Since they hadn't been able to get any proof of murders committed by Ladd himself, he'd gotten off with a lighter sentence of only a few years.

The next bit had caught the attention of Victor's group, though.

This Ladd Russo guy seemed to have an obsession with Huey Laforet, and he'd apparently let slip to other prisoners that he was going to kill him.

"Uh... If I remember right, Huey Laforet was on Ladd's mind back when we picked him up by the rails, too."

"What's this hitman's beef with Huey? It doesn't look like they've ever met... Is it because the Lemures kneecapped his train robbery, so now he hates their boss? Heard some of his pals died, after all," Victor mused, then stuck a note that said *Watch this guy* on Ladd's photo. "Anyway. Tomorrow he gets out of jail."

At that bombshell, the agents exchanged looks.

"He may try to make contact with Huey, or maybe Huey will get interested in the guy who's trying to kill him. Tomorrow, I want several of you on duty watching this fella." Victor paused as something else came to his mind. "Huh. All else aside, the guy's a hitman. Even if it's got nothing to do with the immortals, keep an eye on him and make sure he doesn't try anything. Keep your identities under wraps as well as you can, though."

Victor was about to wrap up his talk there, but Donald interrupted from the sidelines.

"'Scuse me, Assistant Director. There's one more bit of information to add to the materials."

"What is it?"

"Tomorrow, *one other related party* is being released from the same prison."

"...? Whozzat?" Victor asked grumpily. He didn't have any idea.

He probably didn't like the fact that there was information he didn't know, but Donald chose not to believe his boss was that petty in favor of the optimistic interpretation that he was enthusiastic about gathering intel. He filled Victor in matter-of-factly.

"Yeah, it's a coincidence that he's getting out on the same day as Ladd Russo, but..."

After a few minutes, Victor thought for a little while on this new information. He was wondering whether this other person who was being released had any connection to Huey's upcoming experiment.

Of course, he couldn't rule out any possibilities. Unfortunately, the number of agents he had was limited.

In the end, Victor decided to disregard the man.

"...I really doubt Huey would mess with that guy anymore. However, just for the first three days, watch him.

"You're gonna be *guarding* him, too."

Chapter 3 No One Picks Up the Nobody When He Gets Out of Jail

The next day A city in New Jersey In front of the police station

"It's an old cliché, and it's probably pointless to say it to you fellas, but...I don't ever want to see you back here."

In the midst of a drizzling rain, a correctional officer was releasing two people he'd escorted from prison to the closest police station.

"...You and me both," one young man answered, shrugging. Overall, he had a gloomy affect; his hair was dyed black, too, but his natural blond roots were showing. That said, he'd pulled on a cap as soon as he stepped outside, so at a glance, people would think the color was natural.

The other, a virile man with a healthy complexion and a left arm that hung limply, responded with a mix of sarcasm and provocation. "Yeah, *you* might not be the one who has the pleasure of my company. Next time I pull something, I bet I'll land in a prison with gallows."

After they'd said their good-byes, the two men turned their backs on the police station.

They'd done their time, and they were both free and clear. They should have been taking their first steps into new lives, starting out with the handful of money they'd earned from their prison labor, but the drizzle that seeped from the gray sky really didn't seem to be blessing their futures.

"So what are your plans, pal?" the healthy man asked.

The man with dyed hair glanced at the other's prosthetic hand, then restlessly scanned the area, paying an odd amount of attention to what was behind him. "Nah… Don't have any."

The tough man thought that behavior was strange, but he went on making small talk. "I didn't see you in the pen."

"…You probably just don't remember. I've been seeing you around for a good long time."

"Yeah? That's bull. You get out of Alcatraz, too?"

Alcatraz.

The moment he dropped that name, the other guy stiffened.

So he's back from "the island," huh?

To ordinary convicts, it was a place to fear: a prison on an isolated island, where vicious criminals, even those who caused trouble while serving their time, ended up. In other words, the guy he was talking to had to be brutal enough to be sent there.

"…Sorry. I lied. I've just got a few things going on."

"Nah, it don't bother me. Everyone's got a shady past. Especially if they were in the pen. Well, my fellow free man, let's be pals until we go our separate ways, eh?" With an unexpectedly breezy air, the tough man raised his left hand, slowly, for a handshake.

When the man with the dyed hair saw the extended hand, his eyes widened as he focused on the rough prosthetic made of iron. The wet metal gleamed dully in the rain.

"The name's Ladd. Ladd Russo. It's a pleasure."

⇔

Watching the two go from the window of the police station, the correctional officer gave a little sigh.

"Still… To think they'd release those two on the same day."

He sensed some sort of fate at work, but he didn't think it was anything important.

He didn't know the details of Ladd Russo's past, and although he'd been informed of the other man's situation, they hadn't told him all that much about it.

"Well, except for what they have in common."

As if to say he'd lost interest, the officer stepped away from the window and started preparing to get back to work.

Because he turned his back to them, he missed something.

When Ladd Russo held out his left hand to the man with dyed hair, that man landed on his keister on the wet ground, then scrambled all the way back to the edge of the street, terrified out of his mind.

⟺

"Whoa, hey, whassa matter? Did I scare you?"

"D-d-did you say 'Russo'...?"

"Ah." Suddenly, the reaction made sense to Ladd. Smiling, he looked down at the man on the ground. This guy had to know about his Family. He might have even known the rumors about Ladd himself.

Still, he's a little too spooked, ain't he?

True, some people would fear him just because he was mafia, but it was pretty rare for someone to be this openly terrified.

Interesting. What's this guy's story?

For the first time, Ladd was deeply intrigued with this fellow. He folded his arms, fixed the man with a look, smiled thinly, and waited for his reaction.

"I—I see. You're here...to bump me off, aren't you?" the man stammered.

"Huh?"

"I never thought they'd send a hitman this way... Dammit! Did you slip the prison some dough? Or the cops? How much?!" He writhed on the ground, his legs flailing. "Okay, all right, I'll do anything! You want money? I'll pay any price you ask! Just don't kill me! There's somebody I have to find! N-no, I mean, there's nobody! Nobody! I misspoke. A-anyway, even if you kill me now, it's not gonna help anything! I'll give you any intel I can, so lemme go!"

The man kept digging his own grave until he finally reached the wall of a bar that stood by the road. Shaking all over, he braced his hands against it and got to his feet.

Ladd watched the pitiful display with amusement—but then, he noticed something. The man was waving his hands around in a panic, and Ladd had a sense that something was off.

The moment he realized what that *something* actually was, the smile on Ladd's face twisted even further.

"Hey now, calm down. If you don't, you'll die."

Using his right hand, Ladd hauled the other ex-inmate up by his collar. The man's feet left the ground so easily, he might as well have been an empty cardboard box.

That strength was overwhelming.

Experiencing that pure, monstrous power immediately brought the man to a realization.

I can't get away.

I'm going to die here.

The desperate certainty made his knees quake.

"P-please. Would you spare my life, at least? C'mon, I'll do anything, okay?!"

"Yeah, sure, sure, don't worry about it!" Thumping him on the shoulders, Ladd completely ignored the man's fear and his pleas for his life. Instead, he asked him a question. "You got somebody coming to pick you up?"

"To p-pick me up? No… Nothing like that. Nobody would want to."

"That's what I figured. If you were a mafia big shot or something, a luxury car probably woulda pulled up to the curb for ya the moment you stepped out of the station." Chuckling, Ladd slung an arm around the guy's shoulders in an overly familiar way. "Look, in the Russo Family, I'm peanuts. The boss treats me like a good-for-nothing nuisance. See? The Russo Family don't like either of us. So let's get along, a'ight?"

In the man's silence, Ladd continued.

"So, lemme ask you again… What's your name, pal?"

The question was a simple one, but it took the man a little while to find his answer. Then, slowly, he told him.

"I'm…"

The name he gave was his real one. He didn't hide anything. He could probably have given an alias, but he chose not to.

He'd realized that, in the face of the power in front of him, there probably wouldn't be much difference between a lie and the truth. Also, he didn't have a shred of the courage it would have taken to struggle against that overwhelming strength.

When Ladd heard the name, he thought for a little while. "It don't ring any bells."

"……?"

"You're a lucky guy. I dunno what you did to the Russo Family, but for now, you don't have to worry about me."

"O-oh… Okay…" He breathed a sigh of relief, thinking he'd escaped with his life. "Then, sorry, but would you leave me alone…? I'm grateful to you for letting me go, but if I'm with you, I might run into other Russo Family men."

The fear in his voice was obvious, and even as he spoke, his eyes darted around restlessly.

"I like it—the way you're all spooked. You've got no clue when you might die. I can see it in your eyes; you understand just how little it would take. You remind me of Who."

"Who's Who?"

"Who's who. My pal. He's just as much of a coward as you."

"I see… You've got friends. I'm jealous." That hadn't been sarcasm. Even through his fear, the other man lowered his eyes with genuine envy. However, possibly because his terror had finally eased up a bit, he regained just a little of his presence of mind and glanced at Ladd. "He's not coming to pick you up?"

"Well, I dunno if he's alive or dead. From what I hear, most of my buddies on that train died or had their elbows checked and got shipped off to other hoosegows."

"Train?"

"You know the Flying Pussyfoot? I thought they buried the whole damn mess. Have you heard any rumors or anything?"

"The Flying...Pussyfoot?" Although it wasn't as dramatic as it had been when he'd heard the name *Russo*, the man's face changed.

"You sure look like you know something," Ladd remarked.

"...N-nah." He promptly averted his eyes and muttered, as if he was talking to himself. "I dunno a thing."

"A minute ago, you said you'd tell me anything I wanted to know if I let you go, remember?"

He froze. *It's no good.* The only impulse in his mind was the one telling him to give in.

It wasn't as if he'd been hurt; Ladd Russo hadn't threatened him in any way. Yet, *he'd fallen into death's abyss once*, and he knew certain things on instinct.

Just like back then, the man in front of him reeked of death. He wasn't the kind of guy a nobody like himself could disobey.

Respecting his instincts and coming to reason, he hung his head like a tame dog. "...All right, I'll tell you. I'll talk. Dammit, why won't you leave me alone?"

"Well, I thought I might need to know about you."

The man with the dyed hair tilted his head, confused and suspicious.

Putting an arm around his shoulders, Ladd smiled at him, almost as if he was a friend he'd known for years. Grinning, clearly enjoying himself, he whispered in the other man's ear: "We're being watched."

"......!"

"Whoa, don't go rubbernecking. Keep your head right where it is. Get me?"

He kept walking shoulder to shoulder with the other man and turned left at a random corner, putting the police station out of sight.

"There were two in a car and three more faking like they were jawing on the street corner. Five of 'em at least. There may a few that are sharper'n that around, too."

"How…did you know that?"

"I took dirty jobs because my uncle asked. You get good at picking up on that stuff, whether you want to or not."

Who's his uncle? Is it Placido?

He wondered, but he couldn't ask. Intensely fearful of both Ladd next to him and the mysterious watchers, the man with dyed hair kept putting one foot in front of the other and taking ragged breaths.

"…So," Ladd continued, "I want to see whether those Peeping Toms are peeping me or you."

They walked on, traveling farther and farther down empty streets. Then, stopping at a spot that was absolutely deserted, Ladd removed his arm from the other man's shoulders.

"Well, still, y'know. I was thinking while we were walking. It just hit me—hard. Time changes people. If somebody goes a long time without killing people, it sands down all his sharp edges. If this is how it's gonna be, maybe I shoulda beaten that little girl to death, even if Firo held me back."

"…?"

Firo? Who's that? he thought, not saying a word. *Beat a little girl to death? No, c'mon, that's not even funny.*

He wondered whether his own instincts were extremely dull. In the threat he'd sensed in Ladd a moment ago, had he completely failed to account for insanity?

"Actually, I didn't really care whether these guys were after me or you."

"Huh?"

Ladd picked up a chunk of brick that was lying on the ground nearby.

It was just about the right size around which to make a fist, and Ladd began fiddling with it.

The next instant, a black car slowly poked its nose around the corner. The man with the dyed-black hair couldn't see the driver's seat. However, when he noticed how the car was moving, he was sure. This wasn't an ordinary car that just happened to be passing through. Whoever was inside was definitely keeping an eye on them.

"That ain't good," he told Ladd. "Let's duck into a bar or someplace for a minute and lose them."

If they're driving like that, they're probably still amateurs at tailing people.

If that's all they've got, and we slip into a crowd, it'll work out somehow.

In that crowd, he'd part ways with Ladd, and maybe they'd go after him instead; he'd be killing two birds with one stone.

That was the plan he'd worked out in his head.

"It's drizzling, but if we use umbrellas, we may be able to trick—Hey… Uh, hello?"

The man realized Ladd hadn't heard a word of his idea. By the time he turned toward Ladd, the other guy already had his arm wound way up, like a baseball pitcher.

"I'll shellac 'em first, and then I'll either ask 'em straight out or kill 'em… Hup!"

He lobbed the chunk of brick. Traveling unbelievably fast, it smashed the car's window.

The crash signaled the start of a crazy ruckus on that little street.

⇔

A city in New Jersey In front of the police station

"Let me tell you a sad, sad story…"

A voice that seemed to match the gray sky echoed in the street, where a steady drizzle was falling.

"Just a minute ago—which is practically now—my brother Ladd took off. They say he's already gone! …I had no idea such a sad story existed! Even my sister didn't tell me that one… Insane… Is this the limit of mankind? Does life hurt this damn bad?!"

"No, uh, why don't we start by looking for him? He might be in a bar around here, and if he's walking to the train station, we'll catch up to him fast."

In response to that disgusted tone, the man kept his sorrowful howls coming. “Oh… Why do people pass one another by this way? It’s because, in the end, we’re all lonely. We’re locked in the shells of our individuality. Air and water and walls and rain get between us, blocking our way! Dammit, if I were Ladd, I wouldn’t have missed him! Could there be a story this sad?!”

As the young man kept on screaming things that made no sense, the passersby hid their faces with their umbrellas to avoid making eye contact or detoured around him and got out of there.

It wasn’t because what he was saying had frightened them.

They’d felt something unsettling in the fact that he was standing—and screaming—on top of a car that was stopped in front of the police station.

Apparently, the car belonged to the man’s companion, who wore a cap and was slumped over the steering wheel as if he was dead tired. Several of their friends, who looked like delinquents, were standing around the car. They were listening to the soliloquy from the roof, and they hadn’t bothered with umbrellas.

The strange orator seemed to be in his early twenties. The coveralls he wore were a blue so vivid it seemed unreal; even in the drizzle, he stood out clearly.

His most striking feature was the enormous wrench he was toying with. He didn’t have a large build, and his wrench was about as big as a woman’s arm. It seemed more like a medieval warrior’s mace than a tool.

The man shook his blond hair, disheveling it to reveal the dull eyes below it, and kept yelling.

“Jun-Jun says that people are connected on an unconscious level. That’s ridiculous… Why ‘unconscious’? I mean, c’mon, if we’re not connected while we’re conscious, what’s the point?! In Asia, they say you can attain nothingness through Zen meditation… I see. Is that how Asians merge with one another? So that thousand-armed Kannon thingy is a statue of five hundred merged humans… Five hundred… Five hundred?! Whoa, Asians are truly amazing!”

That was when the man started spinning the wrench. The abnormal way he handled it created the illusion that his arms had actually multiplied. When it looked almost as though he'd become a thousand-armed Kannon himself, the guy's melancholy face abruptly lit up...although his eyes were still dull and warped.

"This is fun... Let me tell you a fun story! Incredible, this is fantastic, Shaft! I've awakened to the mysteries of the East! Once five hundred people are merged, they know how to split just their arms... There's not much point in splitting legs, but you can never have too many arms! Jun-Jun's collective unconscious is so perfectly rational!"

The man shouted his ramblings as if they were the truth of the world. Meanwhile, Shaft stuck his head out the driver's side window. "Uh, look, I don't even know where to start demolishing this, but here goes. For starters, the collective unconscious isn't something simple like 'people being telepathically linked.' And is Jun-Jun supposed to be Jung the psychologist? There's no way you've met that guy, right, Mr. Graham? Maybe don't use nicknames for people you've never even seen?"

These were extremely valid points, but the man—Graham Specter—seemed to have cherry-picked a new cause for excitement out of them.

"A nickname... That's it! If we're going to unite, we should start with our names! Okay, from now on, my nickname is Shaft, and my brother Ladd's nickname is Graham! Yours is 'my brother Ladd'! Excellent, what an incredible system. I just might have ended the old world and created a new one!"

"Hello? Come back to us, Mr. Graham. Mr. Graaaaaham!"

"A toast, Shaft! No, wait, Shaft is me! A toast, my brother Ladd! Okay, let's hurry and go look for my brother Graham, whom we managed to miss! Wait, but Graham is my real name! I see, so I was here the whole time... Meaning I didn't pass myself! Am I even supposed to be here?!"

"Definitely not. Let's go find Mr. Ladd already." Shaft was running out of patience, but he hung in there trying to talk with Graham.

Ladd Russo's sworn brother, Graham Specter, led a band of delinquents originally from Chicago. However, due to Graham's personality, the group's members got yanked around on a daily basis, and every time, their subleader Shaft had to calm the situation down. That said, even if Shaft tried to live up to his name and become the axle on which the group turned, Graham was the engine. His torque was too great, and in most cases, it broke Shaft's spirit.

Graham's brain was running full throttle again today, and he didn't seem to be listening to Shaft. "My brother Ladd is suggesting that we go look for my brother Ladd… I see! So this is a journey to find ourselves! Don't worry, Shaft—I mean, my brother Ladd! If we make my second nickname 'my brother Ladd,' our search for ourselves will be completely—"

"Aaaaaaaaaaaaah, it's hopeless. This guy's been hopeless for a while now, and it never changes…"

Things were going the way they always went, and Shaft dropped his head onto the steering wheel again, ready to lose his mind.

Even so, the situation was a little different today.

"Graham," said a clear voice.

It almost seemed to belong to the surrounding drizzle: It was quiet and gentle, and it slowly soaked into their hearts.

"If you let yourself get rained on…you'll catch cold… Get into the car, please."

A young woman was sitting in the backseat. She smiled softly.

"…Yes'm. Thank you, Miz Lua." Nodding obediently, Graham sprang down from the car, opened the passenger-side door, and climbed in.

"Why do you always listen to Lua, Mr. Graham?" Shaft asked.

"Well… Somehow, when I look at her, I start feeling bad. Like I'm getting excited and leaving everyone else behind. Oh, I'm terrible… I'm a lousy, awful, terrible, tactless jerk…"

Like a marionette whose strings had been cut, Graham covered his face with his hands and curled up in the passenger seat.

"It's all right," said the voice from the backseat. "I'm jealous…of all that energy you have, Graham."

"No, uh, sorry, Lua," Shaft said, "but you're only making it worse. Don't do that to him, please."

"My… I'm sorry…" Her voice was gentle, but so faint it could have belonged to a fading ghost. Even so, it echoed strongly in their hearts. That was probably because she was so sincere, despite the volume.

With that thought in mind, Shaft examined the woman's reflection in the rearview mirror.

Lua Klein was engaged to Ladd Russo, the man who'd been released from prison that day. She was also the person that homicidal maniac had publicly declared he'd kill last.

She was beautiful, certainly, and reminiscent of a fairy-tale princess slumbering in the depths of a lake. She seemed far too frail, but Shaft knew she had her own kind of strength, which was directly linked to her weakness.

This lady can accept just about anything.

Even as she watched Graham's abnormal speech and actions, she'd stayed calm and remained true to her own view on life. Apparently, Graham wasn't great with this woman. He often said that looking at her made him aware that he wasn't reading the room. Shaft wished he'd have that same realization when he was dealing with him and the rest of the group.

However, Shaft had also noticed that Lua was a little different. Her fiancé was a murderer, and she was held prisoner by the mafia—but she accepted all those negatives equally.

Shaft had heard that she'd originally wanted to kill herself. It made him wonder just how bad a tragedy would have to be to make a woman like her consider dying.

It wasn't as if she was desperate and self-destructive. She could accept everything, then face it squarely. When Shaft had casually complimented Lua by telling her so, she'd slowly shaken her head and said, "There are things that scare me, too. I realized as much on that train… That monster… The Rail Tracer… It wasn't that I was afraid of the monster. I was afraid…that the monster would kill Ladd…"

Well, that's damn romantic, Shaft had thought, but he also considered Ladd Russo, the one who'd inspired that intensity, to be pretty abnormal as well.

A woman who wanted to die and a homicidal maniac—the

combination seemed like the theme for a comedy skit. Anyone who laughed at their relationship would end up wishing they'd never been born a second later, though.

At any rate, Shaft didn't know what to do with a depressed Graham, so he wanted to reunite Lua with Ladd Russo on the double. Then they could head back to New York, where their group was currently based. "Well, I'll head toward the station first. Even Mr. Ladd can't be planning to hoof it all the way back to New York."

"Naïve… That's naïve, Shaft. Sure, Ladd probably won't walk back…but he's got even more screws loose than I do. He may be making his way using some method we'd never even dream of…" Graham muttered, his face still buried in his hands.

"Yes, yes. He's probably flying there as we speak."

Soothing Graham as if he were a baby, Shaft started the car.

The other members of their crew had taken the train here, and they set off for the station on foot. Shaft pulled out onto the broad avenue, heading from the police station to the train station.

But just a dozen or so seconds later, he spotted something weird.

Farther down the street, a car appeared around a corner and came toward them, weaving from side to side.

"Whoa, what the heck? That's not safe. Is he drunk, or…? Huh?"

Then Shaft saw a peculiar sight. The windshield of the oncoming car was smashed up, and something was clinging to its roof.

Realizing that the clinging "something" was a person he recognized, Shaft grimaced.

Ladd Russo had punched through the car's roof with his prosthetic left arm, then grabbed a slim man by the back of his collar with his right arm, hauling him up.

The iron arm that had slammed down right beside him seemed to have panicked the driver. Both he and the man in the passenger seat were yelling and trying to draw their guns, but just then, the arm abruptly withdrew.

As they tried to see what had happened, the car crashed into the gate around a house, and the impact knocked both driver and passenger unconscious.

Shaft was staring in shock at the nearby accident when Ladd, who'd bailed right before the crash, came over to them. He was dragging a man with his right hand.

He peeked in through the driver's side window. "Hey, we're trying to hitch a ride. Got any empty se—" At that point, Ladd's eyes went to the backseat, and his words caught in this throat. "...Lua?"

Oh, good, he noticed.

Ladd couldn't believe his eyes. Shaft kept his silent relief to himself.

Phew. And actually, I guess he didn't recognize me.

"...Ladd?" Lua also seemed startled by the encounter, which had been far too abrupt—but Shaft didn't have time to let them have their touching reunion.

What was the deal with that accident? Who was the man Ladd was dragging? Shaft had a ton of questions, but for now, he decided the first thing he needed to do was get Ladd into the car and scram.

"Yes, yes, Mr. Ladd, Miss Lua, save the reunion for later, okay?! Let's beat it before the cops...get...here?"

Even as he was speaking, Shaft saw something completely insane.

Before he was aware of it, Graham had gotten out of the passenger seat and was now in the act of bringing that enormous wrench down on Ladd.

What the hell is he doing?!

"Laaaaaaaaaaaaaaaaaaadd!"

The wrench swung down, accompanied by a scream. However, just before it made contact, Ladd turned back, let go of the man he'd been dragging, and caught the weapon firmly with his right hand. As the wrench trembled with tension, Ladd checked to see who was holding it, then gave a startled laugh. "Whoa... Whoa-ho-hoooaaa! If it ain't Kid Graham! Man, it's been forever!"

"How fun... I've got a fun story for you...! It's really you, Ladd!

You stopped a lethal attack easily! One-handed! You really are the genuine article!"

"Wow, hey, if you'd had the wrong guy, he'd be dead." Laughing merrily, Ladd pulled his right arm back, then began turning around, right in the middle of the road.

Graham didn't let go of the wrench, which meant he began traveling in circles, in a move like a giant swing. Ladd's power was monstrous.

"Ha-ha-ha! This is fantastic! My man Ladd really is somethin' else, huh, Shaft!"

"Shaft…? Oh, right! Shaft, Shaft! The fella in the driver's seat!"

Still smiling, after a few more rotations, Ladd gave Graham an extra boost of momentum and let go. Graham flew all the way to the roof of a single-story house by the side of the road, but he flipped nimbly, made a clean landing, then began yelling and brandishing his wrench.

What is this, a circus? Shaft was thoroughly disgusted, but he'd also been reminded why he was afraid of Ladd's strength, which hadn't changed a bit.

This bizarre sight had turned the knees of most of the people on the street to jelly, but as Lua slowly got out of the backseat, she was as calm as ever. She'd never doubted Ladd would come home safely, and as always, she'd accepted everything. The ridiculous scene that had just played out and the way Ladd seemed completely unrepentant even after doing time—Lua had accepted it all.

With a weak smile, she spoke as if they'd only been apart for a day. "Welcome home, Ladd."

"Sorry to keep you waiting, Lua."

Ladd pulled her into a tight hug, confirming that she wasn't an illusion.

As long as you didn't think about what was going through their heads, you could have called it a beautiful reunion, but all Shaft wanted was to get out of there—now.

Just then, Shaft spotted the blue coveralls again. Graham had gotten down from the roof while everyone's attention was elsewhere, and he was poking at the man on the ground with his wrench. "Hey, Ladd? Who the heck is this guy? What's his story?"

"Hmm? ...Oh! I totally forgot. That's my new pal. We got out of the clink together. We hit it off."

"Uh, sure, but his eyes are rolled back, and he's out cold..." Thinking he'd load the guy into an empty space in the car, Shaft climbed out of the driver's seat and took a good look at his face.

Hmm?

Then he noticed something.

The man had worn flesh-colored makeup on his face, but between the rain and the impact, it was nearly gone. From beneath it, old, faint burns had emerged. From the look of those burns and his scars, he might have been caught up in an explosion at one point.

On top of that, *his right hand appeared to be a prosthetic.* It wasn't a rough one like Ladd's left arm, but when he examined it closely, it was obviously a false hand.

The man's face seemed vaguely familiar. As he examined it, Shaft went still for a little while, but then—

From behind him, Graham asked the question straight-out. "So what's this guy's name, Ladd?"

Ladd answered easily. The name he gave was one Shaft *knew*, in a sense.

That said, he didn't remember it as he heard it, and it would be a little while before it all came back to him.

"This guy's Nader. Nader Schasschule.

"It sounds like he's an enemy of my uncle Placido, so I'm gonna hide him."

Chapter 4 There's No Tomorrow for the Kids

Turning back the clock to the rookies' lecture...

Nader Schasschule was a former member of the Lemures, Huey Laforet's personally trained organization, and he'd been trusted with a decent position at a young age.

However, right before the Flying Pussyfoot incident, he'd tried to sell the group out. He'd planned to rub out Goose Perkins, who'd been their leader since Huey's arrest; take the remainder of the organization; and sign on as a subsidiary of the Russo Family.

Someone had snitched on him, though, and his plot had come to nothing. As a traitor, he'd had his right hand cut off, then been blown up with the Lemures' discarded hideout, disappearing under the rubble with the other executed turncoats—or so it had seemed.

Nader had managed to live through the explosion—barely—by using the corpses of several of his comrades to shield himself. That said, he'd sustained injuries he never could have survived on his own. A passing doctor had happened to see the explosion and had saved him. It was practically a miracle.

After that, he'd cut a deal with Victor's men, who were on the Lemures' trail, and received a clean slate in return.

But that wasn't the end of the story.

Nader had disappeared, saying he was going back to the country to farm his father's corn fields.

A few days later, he'd been back at the then-Bureau of Investigation.

He'd told them that someone was trying to kill him. He wanted them to protect him, even if that meant putting him in jail.

"So we were feeling merciful and decided to protect the guy, so we ended up giving him room and board in prison for three whole years, on our own dime? Yeah, come to think of it, I did get a report about something like that. Okay, I see. So that was Nader, huh?"

Finally seeming to have remembered the information clearly, Victor shrugged. "We'd been babysitting him for three years, so we talked him around and shooed him out… Is that how it went? Right, okay."

Bill handed him another report. "Uh… The fact that he and Ladd were released at the same time seems to have been a complete coincidence."

Victor read it in silence for a little while before saying, "Well, enough about Nader or Cider or whatever that zero's name is." With a deep sigh to say the man was no longer on his radar, he switched gears and steered the conversation back to the group he'd tagged with the number seven. "So this gang of delinquents in New York—there's one major thing that sets them apart from the crowd."

"What do you mean?" one of the new guys asked, dubious.

While it was true that they'd been involved in quite a few incidents, they didn't seem to be backed by an organization, and they also didn't appear to be Huey Laforet's guinea pigs.

"Right now, we're just keeping an eye on them, so we haven't messed with them…but the doll who goes around with them is a problem." Sounding irritated, Victor stuck a photo onto the blackboard.

They'd already seen this photo in the materials, but when they looked at it again, the newbies—particularly the younger men—gulped.

Even in a photo taken from a distance, the girl was beautiful. Her lustrous raven hair and vivid yellow-gold eyes matched the features of Huey Laforet, the man behind all the incidents.

Chané Laforet.

She was Huey's daughter. As a long-time member of the Lemures, she'd conducted maneuvers that seemed far too dynamic for a young girl.

It had been four years since the Flying Pussyfoot incident.

The girl who'd cut people down without turning a hair had grown up. The idea of just how terrifying she might have become had concerned the agents, but the remark that she was going around with a group of delinquents filled their minds with questions.

"There was nothing about her in the materials we were given beforehand..."

"Actually, how did you manage to take that photo?"

As the newbies peppered him with questions, Victor adjusted his glasses. "We thought she might be connected with another of Huey's outfits, so we let her walk. Except we ended up just leaving her on the loose, and then Huey busted out of jail! What the hell is that, huh?! Are we idiots?!"

Bill cut in. "Mm... Frankly, you've lived for three centuries, sir. I think the patience that allowed her to go free for three years was very typical of someone such as yourself. As an aside, that photo's a reprint developed from the negative of a photo the delinquents took to celebrate something or other."

Turning his back on Bill, who'd covered for him rather sarcastically, Victor quietly looked up at the ceiling.

"A reprint, huh...? This is a good time to be alive. Back when they first invented photos, that sort of thing couldn't be done. Thanks to a great Talbot, creator of the Talbot process—you know, the 'negative-positive' thing—William Henry Fox Talbot, we're able to share the same photo like this. Be grateful to the name of Talbot, men."

"Uh... Your last names are the same by sheer coincidence. You aren't related or anything, right, sir?" Bill remarked.

Stubbornly ignoring him, Victor turned the conversation back to Chané. "Huey Laforet doesn't think of this girl as his kid. At most, she's an irreplaceable tool for his experiments. If he needs her for the one that he's planning to run, he's bound to come pick her up. If he doesn't need her, he probably won't even stop in to see her." Victor smacked a hand onto the blackboard. "However, from her perspective, it's a very different story. To Chané Laforet, Huey is everything. She practically worships him."

They hadn't collected much intel on her in advance, but an analysis of what they did have suggested they could safely consider her a marked fanatic. It actually made the fact that she hadn't tried to save Huey more of a mystery—but they assumed she hadn't been able to pinpoint where in Alcatraz he was being kept, thus rendering her unable to take action.

"Still… With an information source like Sham and Hilton, there's no way she wouldn't have known. Does this mean Huey's subordinates aren't a monolith?"

"Also, there's one thing that concerns me," Donald said, abruptly joining the conversation.

"What is it?"

Donald pointed to part of Chané's photograph. He was indicating a man's arm, which was slung over her shoulders. "This man who's next to Chané with his arm around her. He contacts her every now and then, but we don't know who he is."

"Does he have ties to Huey?"

"No clue. When Chané does stuff in town on her own, away from that group of delinquents, this fella's with her most of the time. We've checked into him, but we can't find a thing. The delinquents call him Felix, but we don't know whether that's his real name or not. I've had men tail him several times, and he always loses them. It's not clear where he lives."

"…I'd love to say 'Lousy incompetents,' but, Donald, I know your men aren't dumb. Meaning this guy's definitely a pro at *something*." After thinking a little, Victor murmured to himself. "In terms of Felixes in New York…there's Felix the Handyman, but…"

Edward responded to that abrupt word. "You know him?"

"Nah, that ain't him. I made contact with a 'Handyman' who was rumored to be active in New York once, someone who'd help out with anything from hits to midnight disappearing acts...but the one I met was a dame. The name's an alias."

"I see..."

"Well, they probably just happened to have the same name. Sorry. I took us off track." Victor looked back at Chané's photo, scrutinizing the face of the man next to her. The guy was wearing a dauntless smile. "Can't say his mug is particularly striking. He doesn't really look like a mafioso, but... He could be a courier or something. We'll have to check into his link to Chané."

"Erm... Aren't they lovers?" Bill said the first thing the photo brought to mind.

Victor snorted. "You think this woman would have a *lover*?! To her, everything but her old man is dirt on her shoes! It only looks like that at first glance because she's using the guy as camouflage for something. Actually, if this... Uh, what color's his hair?"

It was a black-and-white photo, so he couldn't be sure about the color.

Donald, who'd seen the man from a distance, filled him in. "It's a rather eye-catching red."

"I see. If this redheaded bastard is Chané's fella, I'll jump off the headquarters building and give you a personal demonstration of how immortals regenerate."

As Victor continued to dig himself deeper, Bill sighed and rolled his eyes. "Uh... I really don't think you should be making careless promises. Hmm... If outsiders saw you, we'd have trouble, so treat these fellas to a round of liquor or something instead, all right?"

"Sure, I'll give 'em all a top-class La Tâche from Romanée-Conti."

Victor sneered, but then his expression abruptly reverted to normal. "Don't go falsifying intel just because you want to drink top-drawer wine, people."

Victor was laid-back enough to ease the tension in the room with jokes.

In the end, he didn't notice a crucial detail.

It was a grainy, black-and-white photograph, so that observation would have been nigh on impossible to make—but at the time the photo was taken, with the man's arm around her, Chané had been blushing faintly.

⇔

The next day New York Millionaires' Row

Even in Manhattan, the high-class residential neighborhood attracted nothing but winners. It was fairly close to Central Park, and the environment was particularly fine. As a brisk wind blew down the street of luxury mansions, a whimpering shriek that completely ignored the ambiance echoed from one of them.

"Ugggh! ...*Hic*... N-no, listen, I'm telling you guys, you can't drink this!"

The source of the shriek was Jacuzzi Splot.

His teary wail was met by the coarse voices of delinquents, which didn't suit the street of mansions any better.

"Why not?"

"Yeah, he's right! It was a present and everything!"

"Miss Eve gave it to us!"

"Hya-haah!"

"Hya-haw!"

Amid the storm of criticism, the young man with the tattooed face cradled the box of wine to his chest as if it were a baby.

About three years and two months earlier, a strange incident had occurred aboard the Flying Pussyfoot. This young guy had been a central figure in that affair; maneuvering between the black-suited terrorists and white-suited murderers who'd swarmed all over the train, he'd pulled off a dramatic train robbery.

However, his tears were no act. He was genuinely frightened by his friends' yells.

It had started ten minutes earlier. Eve Genoard, the head of the family who owned the second residence where their group was lodging, had told them, "A wealthy Italian who's been a family friend since my grandfather's time has given me several bottles of fine wine." She'd passed three of those bottles along to Jacuzzi's group.

Jon had brought out a corkscrew, planning to break into a bottle immediately, but Jacuzzi had said "W-wait a second!" before snatching the box away and hunkering down in a corner of the room. "Let's not drink this right this minute, okay?"

The delinquents had been looking forward to tasting this "fine wine," whatever that was. Jacuzzi's suggestion had earned him a barrage of criticism—and in just a few seconds, their young leader had started to cry.

"Okay, okay, just calm down, Jacuzzi. The rest of you, too. Cool it. All right?" said Jon, who used to be a bartender. At least for the moment, the delinquents stopped yelling.

"And? Why shouldn't we drink it? Are you planning to hang onto it until we eat?"

"Huh? N-no, um..."

"Then what's the deal?"

When Jon pressed him, Jacuzzi responded timidly.

"Umm... I thought I'd find someone who'd pay a lot of money for it."

At that remark, the angry yells were loud enough to echo off the walls.

"Huuuuuuuuuuuuuuuuuuuuuuuuh?!"

"Hey, whoa, I guess something's finally gone wrong with my ears!"

"From the way Jacuzzi said that, it almost sounded like he was gonna *sell* that booze!"

"Nah, couldn't be!"

"There's just no way!"

"It's a present from someone who's taking care of us...and he's gonna sell it?"

"Whoa, c'mon, we obviously didn't hear him right. Does our Jacuzzi look like a moneygrubbing ingrate?"

"If he really said that, I'd be sooo disappointed!"

"Yeah, we'd have to give up on him."

"It looks like we've been overestimating Jacuzzi."

"What's this, what's this? Jacuzzi, you've been silent for forty-three seconds already."

"Hya-haah."

"Hya-haw."

As all his friends condemned him, Jacuzzi trembled for a little while. "I—I—I know that! I know! I know better than anyone how lousy I aaaam! Ngh...*hic*..."

Jacuzzi managed the neat trick of getting mad at himself while crying, which temporarily shut the delinquents up. They were aware that, if he went one step beyond this state, Jacuzzi would end up what they called rage-crying.

When Jacuzzi's back was against the wall, even though he kept crying, he sometimes did things that were completely insane. The last time they'd seen him rage-cry, Jacuzzi had grabbed a tommy gun and filled the Russo Family gambling dens with lead, wailing the entire time.

That was why they'd had to make tracks out of Chicago and begin new lives in New York.

"...All right, we get it, just calm down, Jacuzzi."

"We went a little overboard there, too. You ain't the worst, Jacuzzi. You're just about as low as it gets, that's all."

"That's not much different."

"Shut yer trap!"

"Hya-haah!"

"Hyaaa."

A little exasperated by his friends—who hadn't genuinely changed their tune, even though they were nervous now—Jon sighed again and turned to Jacuzzi. "Never mind. Quit crying, Jacuzzi. Tell us what's going on, from the top."

Jon kept his cool because he understood that Jacuzzi wasn't the type to sell presents from other people out of personal greed. The other delinquents had to know that, too. They'd probably just given in to their desires to drink the wine and pick on Jacuzzi.

Jacuzzi slowly said something important, although he was still hiccupping. "The thing is...*hic*...the money, our money, it's...*hic*... It's all gone."

The money was gone.

Due to its very simplicity, that extremely point-blank sentence promptly sent a stir through the delinquents.

Jon's face clouded over, and he pressed Jacuzzi further. "Gone? Did you use it on something?"

"N-no! There's a recession, so...*hic*...the people in town, they don't have...jobs...and so, the odd jobs we picked up earlier just aren't coming in anymore..."

As he spoke, his voice gradually grew quieter. Finally, when even his sobs were subdued, Jacuzzi averted his face from his friends and hit them with the bottom line.

"...So it looks like...we aren't going to be able to make our payment to the Martillos...this month...*hic*!"

⟺

In a bedroom on the mansion's second floor

Although there were multiple guest rooms, the women of the group used this one as their bedroom. Nice, the room's main tenant, was relaxing on a bed. She could hear the yelling and crying from downstairs, but she decided to ignore them.

Just then, there was a knock at the door, and a moment later, Nick came in. "Miz Nice, I dunno why, but they're making Jacuzzi cry again downstairs."

"Yes, it does sound that way."

"He was making some sort of fuss about money..."

Nick, puzzled, was taking the story with a grain of salt. Nice gave him a faint, wry smile. "I imagine it's about not being able to make our payment to the Martillo Family."

"Huh?! Wha—?! That's bad news, ain't it?!"

Their gang of delinquents was basically freeloading off Eve Genoard's family.

Jon and Fang were paid for the housekeeping they did, but naturally, it wasn't possible to keep a large number of delinquents fed on an income like that. Several people had been picking up side jobs and earning pocket money, but they'd done this on turf belonging to the Martillo and Gandor Families without permission, which had ended up getting them marked by both outfits. After various twists and turns, in the end, it had been decided that they'd make regular payments to the Martillo Family.

"The recession has significantly curtailed our income recently. After all, since Prohibition ended and the speakeasies started to operate openly, even underworld businesses have begun to really feel the Depression."

"They're getting hit hard, too, huh… What'll we do, Miz Nice? If we end up stiffing them, who knows what that freaky magician will do to us?"

The "freaky magician" was Ronny Schiatto, a Martillo Family executive. Ever since a certain incident earlier in the year, the delinquent group's image of him had been *We don't know what the hell is up with him, but he's a magician and really scary.* Fortunately, everything had worked out that time, but if they ended up not being able to make their payment, there was no telling what might happen to them.

The situation really was terribly dangerous, but Nice didn't look all that worried. "It's all right. If it comes to that, I'll do something about it."

"What kind of something?"

"It will hurt, but I'm prepared to sell myself off, piece by piece."

It was a shocking declaration, and Nick hastily tried to dissuade her. "Whaaat?! You can't do that! Anything but that, Miz Nice! If you're going 'cause you want to, that's one thing, but if you do that sort of work with a gang, they'll get their hooks into you and trap you…"

"What are you talking about, Nick?"

"Huh?"

Nick frowned, and Nice cocked her head, perplexed. "I only meant I'd sell them the bombs I have on hand."

"Huh?! B-but you said 'sell myself off, piece by piece'…"

"My bombs are part of me. Or maybe they're more like my children!"

"Please don't blow up your kids!"

Nick had retorted on momentum, but even as he spoke, something struck him as odd. "Uh… Miz Nice? You've got a bomb that's enough to cure our money troubles? …Where?"

He knew Nice always had explosives of some sort on her person, but those would probably only go for a song. A nasty feeling raced up his spine, but Nick asked the question anyway.

Hey, whoa, come to think of it, the closet in here is pretty big… Miz Nice isn't the type to buy a ton of clothes for herself.

N-no… It couldn't be, right?

Nick glared at the closet, breaking out in a cold sweat. Ignoring him, Nice got up from the bed, her eye shining—and yanked the sheets and the thin pad from the mattress.

"Yaaaaugh?!"

Nick screamed and backed up all the way to the wall.

The space under the bed was jammed with a cornucopia of bombs.

"Wha…? A-a-are you outta your mind, Miz Nice?!"

Nice looked away sadly. She sounded just a little apologetic. "…I'm sorry, Nick. You're correct that storing gunpowder this way damages it, but…even so…the temptation to sleep on top of them was irresistible!"

"Uh, the storage method ain't the problem! The problem is where you're storing it!!" Managing to hang onto his wits, Nick protested. "C'mon, I was scared enough as it was, and you just made it worse! I just assumed you had 'em in the closet!"

"Chaini's, Melody's, Chané's, and Rail's clothes are in there as well, so that wouldn't work. Besides, closets are for storing clothes, you know, not bombs."

"Yes, I know that!" Nick snapped, clinging desperately to common sense. "Listen, if a fire broke out, you'd be blown to bits instantly! *You* would, Miz Nice! You'd be the first to go!"

"I would…be blown to bits…by these little ones…?" As she

visualized the scene and faced the idea of her own death, Nice looked down, her cheeks flushing a little.

"Why are you blushing?! That ain't right, Miz Nice!"

As a rule, Nice Holystone was a sensible person. It was, of course, relative to the others in their group, but she was generally the one who scolded her friends when they got out of control. She also got through to Jacuzzi when he was confused.

However, she also possessed one of the least commonsense aspects of the entire group.

Bombs: tools capable of absolute destruction.

Nice was a dyed-in-the-wool bomb fiend who took pleasure in the shock wave, the flash, and the roar of bombs, and in the smell of burning gunpowder. When it came to bombs, and only then, her mental screws had a tendency to come loose. Nick had watched her for long years—although not as long as Jacuzzi had, since he'd been her childhood friend—and he'd thought he was very familiar with that tendency of hers. And yet when he actually saw the mountain of bombs—unsurprisingly, he couldn't keep his cool.

"You seriously still have all this…? Does Jacuzzi know?"

"If I told him about them, he'd sprint right out of the mansion, don't you think?"

"I feel like doing that myself." Nick had finally calmed down.

As Nice put the mattress back in place, she asked a question of her own. "By the way, what was the matter? Didn't you need something? I really can't imagine you'd come up here just to tell me Jacuzzi was crying."

"Huh? Oh yeah! Yeah, that's right! Right, Miz Nice! Stop Jack, wouldja?!"

"Jack? What's wrong?"

Jack was an older member of the group, one Nice had known about as long as she'd known Nick. What on earth was he attempting to do? Before she could ask, Nick yelled the answer.

"That bastard's planning to die!"

⟺

A few minutes later In another room of the Genoard mansion

"Don't you stop me. I'm serious here."

A punching bag stuffed with rags hung from the ceiling.

In Japan, where such bags are more likely to be filled with sand than rags, they're known as sandbags. As Jack spoke to the friends who stood behind him, he was slugging this one rhythmically.

"You mean to do this no matter what, Jack?" Nice's voice was grave.

Jack responded without even looking at her. "Yeah. I won't rest until I've laid that Ladd Russo asshole out with my own two hands."

Ladd Russo and the gang of delinquents had a little history between them.

Of course, Jacuzzi's group and the Russo Family had been enemies before, so you could say the conflict had always been there, but new trouble had broken out from the Flying Pussyfoot incident.

When Jack had been taken hostage by the group of people in black suits, Ladd Russo had worked him over on a whim and had left him so badly injured he'd almost died. Luckily, since a doctor had happened to be on the train with them, he'd survived, but if he hadn't received medical help, he might not have made it. Jacuzzi had declared they'd "*make Ladd pay for it*," cementing their hostile relationship.

Strangely, though, Ladd and the other white suits had vanished from the train. They'd suspected the group had been wiped out by the Rail Tracer, who was rumored to have been on board. From there, though, the story got even more complicated.

"Yeah, but Graham said he'd mediate for us...," Nick said.

Graham Specter was Ladd's sworn younger brother. He'd taken a shine to Jacuzzi's group after a certain incident and had been looking out for them ever since. From what he said, Ladd Russo had gotten arrested before. His prison term was up today, and Graham and the woman to whom Ladd was engaged had gone to get him. They were probably meeting up in New Jersey right about now.

Graham knew about the feud between the Russo Family and Jacuzzi's gang, and so he'd offered to be their mediator: "Okay, got it, I'll introduce you to Ladd as my pals. It'll be fine. Ladd never kills somebody once he's decided you're his pal… Probably. It hasn't happened so far anyway!"

However, Jack still wasn't satisfied with that arrangement. "So what if he's Graham's sworn brother? That changes nothing!" he yelled. "Listen, not a day goes by when I forget I almost bit the big back then!"

"I understand how you feel, Jack. To be honest, even if Graham mediates for us, I'm not eager to form a connection to that Ladd fellow."

"Then why are you trying to stop me?"

"As I'm telling you, *I don't want to have a connection to him*, friendly or hostile."

Her argument was so sound there was no way to respond to it. Jack pressed a fist against the punching bag. "…In that case, I can't cause trouble for you or Jacuzzi, Nice. Nick and I will do it."

"Why are you dragging me into this?!"

"Tch…! You were there, too. How come you got off without a scratch?"

"What, you're *jealous*?!" Nick screamed.

Jack flashed him an amused grin. "Kidding. I'll do it myself."

"Oh, you were just fooling, huh…? No, wait! C'mon, Jack, tell me getting revenge on Ladd was a joke, too! Listen, there's no way you can beat that crazy bastard. Right?"

As a matter of fact—although, granted, he had been hit first—Jack hadn't been able to touch Ladd. Frankly, as an amateur, he didn't think even training constantly for a few years would have guaranteed him a win. On top of that, he'd only started slugging that punching bag a few days ago, when he'd heard Ladd Russo's sentence was up.

"It's not about whether I can win or not. That guy shredded my pride! If I don't step up here, I'll never be able to throw another punch!"

"If you want to pretend you're as cool as a boxer, that's fine, but c'mon: 'I went to rob a train, then got clobbered by a passing murderer, so I'm taking my revenge…' That's just pathetic."

"Sh-shaddup!"

Jack had always been ready to fight at the drop of a hat, and this was definitely like him. Still, they couldn't let this situation slide.

"Nick, call Jacuzzi, Donny, Jon, and Fang, please."

"Huh? Yes'm." Nick headed out of the room.

As he watched him go, Jack frowned. "H-hey, what gives? You better not be planning to sit on me and tie me up."

"If I were, Jacuzzi would be useless, so I wouldn't have called him," Nice casually replied, although it was a mean thing to say. She sighed, then went on slowly. "They're the others who were on the train with us. I'd like to call Chané as well, but I imagine her history with Ladd would complicate things."

Nice was remembering the violent death match she'd seen between Chané and Ladd Russo on the roof of the train. She hadn't asked Chané what had happened between them. However, she'd noticed the other woman had been acting strange ever since Ladd Russo's name had come up a few days ago.

It isn't just Jack. I'll have to talk with Chané later, too.

...Before Graham and the others bring Ladd here.

Even as she internally planned her next steps, Nice went on talking to Jack. "Listen to me. As I told you, we're all in the same boat regarding that train robbery. We may not be on the train anymore, but that part hasn't changed."

Jack said nothing.

"That being the case, if you insist on taking revenge, we'll assist you. It's quite likely that he'll kill all of us instead. No doubt it will end Graham and Jacuzzi's hard-earned friendship as well."

"N-no, like I said, don't bother about me..." Jack faltered, averting his eyes.

Interrupting him, Nice spoke firmly. "You know we can't leave you to do this alone. Not me, not the rest...and certainly not Jacuzzi."

"Ugh..." Jacuzzi's face rose in his mind, and Jack looked down guiltily.

"No matter how reluctant he is at first, in the end, Jacuzzi will help you with your revenge. Even if it means showing ingratitude toward Graham. Even if it endangers his own life."

"...So what are we gonna do, then?"

"We'll talk it over together. Those of us who were on the train will discuss what to do next."

"...That's dirty, Miz Nice. If you tell me that, I've got no choice but to back down."

Gently swearing under his breath, Jack thumped a fist into the punching bag.

A bomb had appeared in Nice's hand at some point during the conversation, and she toyed with it while she smiled kindly at Jack. "It's all right, Jack. If this Ladd fellow decides to squander Graham's mediation and picks a fight with us...then I'll strike before you do."

There were two basic factors behind Nice's smile. One was the resolution to get her hands dirty for her friends' sake. The other was simply a bomb fiend's thrill at having the opportunity to blow something up.

Jack was well aware of this, and he gave a wry smile. "That ain't actually all right."

Noticing the urge to kill had faded from his face, Nice felt relieved. *Now,* she thought, *as long as we talk it over with Jacuzzi and everyone else, there won't be any problems.*

But when Nick returned to the room, he brought a new problem with him. "Miz Nice, it sounds like Jacuzzi left with Rail and some other people."

"He left? Where did he go?"

Jacuzzi had been bawling just a few moments ago. Where on earth could he have gone?

"Well, the thing is, Isaac and Miria apparently stopped by." Nick's expression was a mixture of confusion and discomfort. "They said they were going to see some guy named Molsa to get work, but... that name kinda rings a bell for me. Who's Molsa again?"

When she heard that name, Nice flinched, froze up, and dropped the bomb she was holding.

"Whoa!!" Jack caught the bomb a second before it could hit the ground.

"I think...," Nice said, breaking out in a cold sweat.

"That's probably...the boss...of the Martillo Family."

⇔

A few minutes earlier The front hall of the Genoard residence

"Hello, hello! Jacuzzi! How've you been? And why do you look like you're about to cry?"

"Yes, crocodile tears! Crying uncle!"

The pair who had come in through the front door were benefactors to Jacuzzi's group.

"By the way, Miria, why are the crocodile and the uncle crying?"

"Maybe they were family who found each other again…"

"I see! So the uncle and the crocodile are father and son, hmm?! I hear, in the mysterious lands of the Far East, ugly ducklings give birth to swans… That means it wouldn't be strange for the crocodile and uncle to be related. It's great that they got back together!" Satisfied by his own explanation, Isaac nodded away. Then he turned to Jacuzzi, who was looking haggard. "So who'd you get back together with, Jacuzzi?"

"Huh? I—I haven't really, not yet… Tomorrow, technically, there's somebody I'm planning to meet again, but…"

Jacuzzi wasn't good with Ladd Russo, either. If they met him and Jack said he was going to get his revenge, he'd end up having to help Jack, so if possible, he wanted to get by without running into Ladd.

Nnngh… And I said something crazy about how I was absolutely going to make him pay someday…

Wh-what'll I do if he remembers?

The anxiety built up, and Jacuzzi almost burst into tears again.

Isaac and Miria peeked at his face and nodded emphatically.

"You're so glad you'll get to see this person again that you're crying. I'm real happy for you."

"Yes, we'll all have to celebrate!"

"Right, let's raise the roof!"

"Mm-hmm, money makes the world go round! Money rolling!"

The pair cheerfully made remarks that were completely oblivious to Jacuzzi's actual state.

"I think you might mean 'money laundering'... A-anyway, Isaac, Miria, I'm sorry! We don't have that kind of money anymore."

Jacuzzi was getting worried that if this kept up, they might actually throw a party, so he bluntly disclosed the state of their finances.

"What, no money? Well, that's perfect! We're broke, too!"

"Yes, we match!"

"There's nothing good about that..." Rather envious of how few worries the pair ever seemed to have, Jacuzzi heaved a big sigh. "Man, what'll we do...? As things stand, that payment to the Martillo Family really isn't going to..."

He'd muttered the words to himself, but they didn't get past Isaac. He glanced at Jacuzzi.

"The Martillos? What's this, Jacuzzi? Did you borrow money from the Martillos?"

"Huh? Oh, n-no, well, something like that."

Jacuzzi didn't want to involve these two in the matter of their regular payments, so he tried to gloss it over.

Isaac smiled at him. "I see. We were planning to ask you if you had any jobs for us, but I guess we're in the same bind..."

"Yes, we're underemployed! The New Deal!"

"Mr. New Deal's got it rough, too, huh!"

It wasn't clear whether they actually understood what *the New Deal* meant. Miria and Isaac pondered the matter soberly for a second, but then their faces lit up, and they grabbed Jacuzzi's arms. "Well then, let's go!"

"Huh? G-go where?"

As they pulled him along, Jacuzzi looked blank. Isaac filled him in, sounding terribly confident.

"We know this restaurant owner named Molsa! He belongs to the Martillos, too, so we'll ask him to wait a while on that loan!"

"Yes, and he might just give you a job!"

"Hey, in that case, do you think he'll have work for us, too?"

"Yaaay, we'll be rich!"

As Isaac and Miria arbitrarily dragged both him and the conversation along, Jacuzzi thought, *What?! He's with the Martillos? C-come to think of it, Isaac and Miria seemed to know that Ronny guy...*

"B-but, Isaac. If you do that, won't it cause trouble for you? Even if we're acquaintances, if you take somebody like me over there and start asking about money, they'll get mad at you..."

Jacuzzi's worry was perfectly natural. Isaac and Miria exchanged looks, then cocked their heads, seeming puzzled.

"Why? If you and your pals do some work, Molsa will get his money back, so he'll be happy, too."

"Yes, happy money! A money ending!"

Isaac genuinely seemed to have no cares at all, while what Miria was saying didn't even make sense.

"B-but..." Jacuzzi was still hesitant.

A child's high-pitched voice cut in. "Hey, Jacuzzi, why not? You'll finally get a chance to talk to them."

When they looked over, they saw a kid who seemed to be about ten years old.

Countless suture scars ran all over their body like railroad tracks, from their face to the tips of their toes. People who were seeing them for the first time would probably get the mistaken impression that someone had tried to draw a picture of some sort, using their body as a canvas.

The owner of this peculiar exterior—who looked like a boy at first glance but was actually a girl—had spoken to Jacuzzi, sounding innocent. Possibly because her eyes were expressionless, the way the sutures pulled up the corners of her lips made it look like she was smiling.

"Rail? Y-yeah... Maybe that's true, but..."

"Except I'd be nervous if it was just you, Jacuzzi, so I'll go along."

Without revealing a fragment of what she really felt, Rail trotted after Jacuzzi.

One of the delinquents spoke up. "Hey, whoa. If you're going, Rail, let's call Miz Nice and we'll all go..."

But Rail shook her head.

"If we all went, they'd have their guard up. If a kid like me is with him, they might be nice, you know? As long as they don't mind a kid who's all scarred up. Ha-ha!"

⇔

Twenty minutes later   In a private room at Alveare

"He… H-he— H-h-h-h-h-h-h…h-hello, it's good to meet you, s-s-s-sir… Eeep…agh…" Jacuzzi was very close to hyperventilating.

The man he was facing spoke to him calmly. "…You okay, kid?"

"Y— Y-y-yessir!"

Jacuzzi was trembling violently. In contrast, the man on the opposite side of the round table at the back of the room was fully composed. His self-possessed bearing made it clear that he was the master of this room and the king of the building. He was probably around fifty or sixty years old, and there was a faint sprinkling of white in his carefully combed hair.

The man nodded, then turned his attention to Isaac and Miria, who sat beside the quaking Jacuzzi. "So, Isaac. It sounds like you've got something formal to discuss here, but who's this kid?"

"Well, he's a friend of ours. His name's Jacuzzi. The thing is, Jacuzzi's borrowed money from somebody in the Martillo Family, but he can't pay it back."

"Yes, he's short on cash! Vanishing gold!"

"So he'd like you to point him toward work of some sort! And while you're at it, point us toward some, too!"

It was an extremely simple explanation.

Even though it was what Jacuzzi had told them a little while ago, the facts didn't quite match what he'd just heard, and his tattooed face turned paler than it ever had before.

"Oho… Money, hmm?"

Lacing his fingers together and resting his hands on the table, the middle-aged man spoke in a grave voice. "Well, let me introduce myself first. I'm Molsa Martillo."

Hearing that name sent another shudder down Jacuzzi's spine.

Th-that's right. I remember. I remember now! Molsa… That's the name of the M-Martillo Family's boss! H-how do Isaac and Miria know somebody this important?!

I—I'm gonna die, aren't I?

R-Rail said she'd wait outside...

H-help meee! Somebody, anybody, save me!

He felt as if he might faint at any moment, but he scraped together what *little* spirit he had and held on, responding in a voice so faint it was barely audible. "I'm J-Jacuzzi...Splot."

"I see. It's a pleasure, Jacuzzi. Firo, a member of my family, owes a great deal to Isaac and Miria. Any friend of theirs is a friend of the Martillo Family."

"Uh-huh..."

He owes them...? I wonder what they did.

Jacuzzi was mystified, but Molsa's voice pulled him back to reality.

"That said, I don't think much of borrowing an amount you can't pay back. Who in this family loaned it to you?"

His voice was mild, but it held a weight that seemed to bear down on the whole room.

Just then—the man who was standing behind Molsa spoke. He was the individual who was responsible for half of Jacuzzi's nerves: Ronny Schiatto.

"Excuse me, *capo masto*. Technically, it was me."

"You, Ronny?"

"This kid's the leader of a group of delinquents who were active on our territory. The year before last, I settled the matter by requiring them to make regular payments to us, but with the Depression... I believe their income is down, and it's become difficult to pay."

At this accurate, impassive description of their situation, Jacuzzi hung his head apologetically.

"I see. And that's why you're looking for work, is it?" Molsa asked him.

Ronny lowered his head in apology. "I'm terribly sorry. I should have handled this matter, but I've forced you to get your hands dirty with it."

Aaaaaaaaaaaaaah! He's sorry?! That scary Ronny guy said he was sorry!

I—I—I—I knew it! Molsa really is a terrifying person!

"Don't talk like that, Ronny. What's dirty is the work we do. I've gotten to talk with one of the town's young people; I'll consider it a valuable experience."

"If you're sure, sir."

Ronny took a step back. Ignoring him, Molsa spoke to Jacuzzi again. "Now, then. That said, protection money isn't the sort of thing we can just casually compromise on...as I'm sure you're aware, Jacuzzi Splot."

"Eeep?! Y-yessir!"

"So what do you intend to do? Which member of your group is going to compensate us, and how?"

"I am." Simply, far too simply, the young man whose eyes had been filled with tears until just then interrupted Molsa. "All the responsibility is mine. So I'll make up for all of it, so please...don't lay a finger on...a-anyone else... I-if possible, I'd rather not die...but..."

The last half of his sentence grew teary again. However, for just a moment, Molsa had picked up on the intense resolution in Jacuzzi's eyes. "Hmm..."

A slight change came over the boss's expression, and he studied Jacuzzi's face as if it intrigued him.

As they watched the two men converse, Isaac and Miria were whispering together.

"This sounds like a pretty complicated conversation, Miria."

"Yes, I bet it's about politics!"

Molsa, who'd picked up on their exchange, grinned from ear to ear. "Yes, it certainly is," he said with some amusement. "Jacuzzi may become a politician someday."

"Huh?!"

The conversation had taken an unexpected turn, and Jacuzzi spoke up, startled. As his eyes darted around in confusion, Isaac and Miria complimented him.

"Whoa, that's really something! Jacuzzi's got a lot of friends, so he might get to be president."

"Yes, Abraham Lincoln! James Garfield! William McKinley!"

"N-no, I couldn't, I could never...ha-ha..."

Jacuzzi's lips softened into a smile; the tension had eased, and he kind of liked the sound of that.

"...All those presidents were assassinated."

At that comment from Ronny, Jacuzzi's face went pale, and he started trembling again.

Nonetheless, Molsa had taken kindly to Jacuzzi. "Never mind that. You're paying us protection money, so we've got a duty to protect your group. That's true even now, regardless of major financial woes."

"Huh? Th-then..."

"I'll give you jobs. If you do them well, you'll be able to earn enough to cover half a year's worth of payments."

"D-do you mean it, sir?! Thank you very much!"

After he'd hastily expressed his gratitude, Jacuzzi suddenly got nervous.

W-wait. What sort of gang-related job would bring in that much?

D-don't tell me... Messengers who aren't expected to come back...? Corpse disposal...? Assassination?!

The more he thought about it, the more dangerous his ideas grew.

Picking up on his unease, Molsa laughed.

"Relax, kid. When all's said and done, I'm still Camorra. I won't make anyone who's not part of my family do anything reckless... Well, the jobs may be reckless in another sense of the word, but..."

"What are you planning to have them do, sir?" Ronny asked.

Molsa grinned in a way that made him look young. "You-know-what is happening next week."

"...I see. You'll have them help with that?"

Although he'd only been told "you-know-what," Ronny nodded as if he was completely satisfied.

"????????" Jacuzzi didn't know what was going on, and his gaze wandered uneasily around the room.

Ever impassive, Ronny asked him a question. "Jacuzzi Splot, do you know the rules of poker?"

"Huh? Um, well...I play it with the other guys sometimes, so..."

"Any experience with roulette? Craps? Blackjack? What about the slots?"

"Huh? No... Almost none... Casinos are scary, so I..."

"Hmm… Well, never mind. How is your luck? Good?"

"I think it's lousy. Oh, but…I'm lucky about getting away with stuff…I guess."

"Do you have tuxedos and dresses? Enough for your entire group, if possible."

"I-if we had that, we would have sold them for cash…"

"Hmm… In that case, I'll provide some for you—*tailored*."

The man kept asking him rapid-fire questions, and Jacuzzi answered as best he could. When the questions and answers had gone on for a little while, after some hesitation, Ronny nodded to Molsa.

"Well, it should be all right," Ronny said. "After all, the fact that they aren't members of our family is excellent."

"True, but they're the sort of jobs that have to be done by people we can trust."

"But you do trust them, don't you, sir?"

"Well, I trust this kid. They say you can tell the quality of a group by its leader."

Jacuzzi wasn't able to follow the conversation; he just listened to them quietly. However, eventually, as if he couldn't take it anymore, he asked a timid question. "U-um… So what is it we'll need to do?"

"Oh, it's easy."

Molsa's answer was extremely simple.

"Gamble."

⇔

A few minutes earlier At the counter inside Alveare

Alveare had originally been a speakeasy that served bootleg honey liquor. Even now that Prohibition had ended and they'd hung their sign out front, their basic concept hadn't changed. In this unique space, the sweet scent of honey had permeated the wooden tables and the floor. The pale light of the incandescent bulbs made the honey in the food shine golden, so that the spacious room resembled the treasure chamber of a pirate ship. Once in a while, the aroma's cloying intensity made a customer get unpleasantly drunk, but most people savored that smell as if it were one of the restaurant's dishes.

In that saccharine space, there was a young woman who left a sharp impression. Her name was Ennis.

She'd just finished helping them unload groceries in the back and was taking a break at the restaurant's counter. She was wearing a black men's suit, which was an uncommon fashion for women in America at the time. It went well with her androgynous beauty, however, and the people around her certainly weren't put off by it.

There were almost no regular customers near her, most likely due to the tacit understanding that the seats close to the counter were reserved for Martillo Family associates. However, Ennis was currently feeling a little bewildered; she'd noticed an unfamiliar child watching her.

The child, who seemed to be about Czeslaw Meyer's age, had taken the seat next to hers and had a face and hands marked with striking suture scars, but even including those, their features were balanced and even.

A boy... No, a girl?

At first, that was the only question on Ennis's mind, but the child watched her so intently that she soon became concerned in a different way. She'd originally thought it was because her clothes were unusual, but when Ennis stole a glance, she noticed the child's gaze seemed to be focused more on Ennis herself than on her clothes.

No one at the counter seats appeared to be the child's guardian. She couldn't imagine they had ties to the Martillo Family, either.

Those eyes kept boring holes into her, and Ennis didn't know what to do. For a little while, she drank her herbal tea with some bewilderment.

"Miss, is your name Ennis?" a young voice abruptly asked.

"Huh...? Yes, it is, but...who are you?"

When Ennis turned, perplexed, she found herself looking right into the child's eyes.

They didn't answer her question and instead examined Ennis's face closely, giving her a *taunting smile.* "Hmm… You're not what I expected."

"?" Ennis didn't understand.

"I thought you'd be burlier, like old Szilard! Ah-ha-ha!"

"…!" She gasped.

Szilard.

The moment she heard that name, Ennis's spine froze. Apprehension rushed over her like a wave.

If this child was somehow connected to Szilard Quates, why come here? For what purpose?

She imagined a worst-case scenario in which the child would consume her and braced herself, preparing to leap out of her chair at any moment.

Even as she stiffened, the child laughed and spoke to her softly. "Oh, c'mon. Don't get so upset with me. I'm a homunculus, just like you."

The words were so quiet that only Ennis could hear them, but they sent another shock through her.

"…!"

"That said, unlike you, I'm—we're—failures… Ha-ha!"

"You're…"

"I heard you were with some group called the Martillo Family, but I had no idea we'd run into each other here. Oh, I'm Rail. Nice to meet you and all that."

A current of tension ran between them.

The surrounding customers hadn't registered the strained mood, and the restaurant was as lively as ever. As a matter of fact, even the new customer who came in didn't spare a glance for Ennis or Rail.

"Excuse me."

The moment the customer spoke to Seina, the proprietress who stood behind the counter, it was Rail's turn to stiffen.

"I heard you could talk to people from the Martillo Family here."

Rail's face had gone blank. Thinking this was odd, Ennis also glanced toward the speaker.

The voice belonged to a child who seemed to be a year or two older than Rail.

Just as Ennis was trying to get a better look at the newcomer, Rail brusquely turned away, as if Ennis didn't matter anymore.

"Hey… Why are you here, hmm?" Rail asked.

The new visitor looked over, blinked a few times, then curtly replied, "…Oh. Rail."

Rail ground their teeth together in frustration, moments away from venting—but when the next man walked in, they stopped dead.

Rail wasn't the only one. The man who'd entered had put the restaurant's lively atmosphere to rest as well.

"Nice. Yeah, very nice!" His voice resonated throughout the establishment. "This place is terrific! Fantastically marvelous and auspicious!"

At the sight of the theatrical man, Rail completely froze.

"What's good about it? Well, the aroma of honey! It's Nature's supreme sweetness! Is everyone in here grateful to the honeybees? Let's see, yes, I'll thank them now!"

The man's teeth had all been replaced with sharp canines that resembled dolphin teeth, and the parts of his eyes that should have been white were completely red. His clearly abnormal appearance made every person in the restaurant tense, with the exception of the child who'd come in just before him.

Ennis remembered the man's face—and she stiffened as well.

That's… Last year, he's the one who…!

Recalling the incident at Mist Wall and suspecting that he might harm the people in Alveare, she quickly stood up. However, before she could break into a run, someone spoke from below her eye level, stopping her in her tracks.

"Chris…" A variety of emotions mingled in their voice to the point where it sounded almost dull-witted. "Christopher…"

The laid-back attitude the child had taken with Ennis was gone without a trace. The moment Rail saw the man's face, the change was obvious.

Large, unmistakable tears welled up in Rail's eyes.

At the sight of those genuine tears, Ennis was so bewildered she couldn't do a thing.

⟺

Meanwhile In a private room

"Gamble…? Huh? What do you…mean…?"

In response to Jacuzzi's uneasy question, Molsa smiled.

"Ah, well, if you want details, just ask… Hmm. Who should I get to explain this?" After thinking it over for a bit, Molsa gave him a man's name. "There's a fella named Firo Prochainezo. He's a little older than you are."

"Uh, uh-huh…"

During the Mist Wall incident, Jacuzzi and Firo had both been in the restaurant on the top floor. However, it wasn't as if they'd introduced themselves or had a conversation, and Jacuzzi had apparently forgotten him entirely.

Come to think of it…haven't Isaac and Miria mentioned a "Firo" quite a lot?

He vaguely remembered that they had, but before he had time to ask them about it, Molsa went on. "He's going to take part in a gambling get-together that's being held in a certain location real soon. He'll be running a section of it. Long story short, I'd like your group to give him a hand."

"…Give him a hand?"

Was he asking them to be dealers? Jacuzzi couldn't even shuffle a deck of cards properly, so there was no way he'd ever manage that. *B-besides…what if somebody loses and starts yelling about clip joints and gets violent…?* Visualizing himself getting throttled by a man about as big as Donny, Jacuzzi felt his entire body turn pale.

"There's nothing to be scared of. All you need—well, all your group needs to do is have fun gambling. Of course, the casino's illegal, so you'll be at risk if the cops raid it, but still."

"……"

This makes even less sense now.

Why would having fun gambling count as a job?

At any rate, he thought, he'd need to hear about this in more detail before he accepted the offer and went forward with it. Jacuzzi was about to ask Molsa another question before he met this Firo guy, but—

He was interrupted by a knock.

"'Scuse us."

"Excuse us, *capo masto*. There's something we need to tell you."

Two men entered the room. One was fat, the other abnormally thin.

"What is it?" their boss asked mildly.

"Well...," said the thin man. "We just got a coupla weird customers. They say they're mafiosi who got run off by their family. They want to sign on under us."

"Become our subordinates? A little outfit like this?" Molsa frowned.

Although the Martillo Family was a small syndicate, it scraped by and defended its own turf without the protection of a larger organization, which was an uncommon practice. If someone wanted to sign on under their small outfit, either they felt a deep obligation to the Martillo Family, or they were ambitious types who planned to infiltrate the syndicate and take over their territory from the inside.

"What syndicate are they from and where? What brought them to New York?" Molsa asked.

If they'd been chased away from their earlier home due to a hostile relationship with a large syndicate, they'd have to be very careful. After all, taking them on as subordinates would mean picking up their obligations and grudges as well.

"No... They're kinda odd... One says he's the boss of the Russo Family."

"R-Russo?!" Jacuzzi screamed.

The boss of the Russo Family, Placido Russo, was the man who'd put a bounty on Jacuzzi's group.

His syndicate had also killed several of Jacuzzi's friends.

Caught between the impulse to take to his heels and another impulse bubbling up beneath the first to settle the score here, Jacuzzi felt his heart struggling not to be crushed.

Molsa couldn't know about the connection between Jacuzzi's

group and the Russo Family, but Jacuzzi's scream and the expression that followed it must have shown the older man that there was history there.

"Relax. I won't let them do anything." Molsa sent Ronny a brief glance.

Understanding everything from that silent look, Ronny responded deferentially. "Understood, sir."

Molsa issued orders to the thin and fat men, who were family executives. "Show our guests in. I'll let them bring one guard, but take their weapons and hold on to them outside the room."

"Yessir! Oh, uh, well, in terms of numbers, I wouldn't worry about it."

"?" Molsa paused.

"It's only the boss and one guard."

After that, Isaac and Miria said, "It sounds like you've got other guests, so we'll wait outside!" and took their leave, but Jacuzzi stayed where he was. He'd decided it would be better to meet them here in the room than run into them in the corridor.

However, even though he'd nearly prepared to die, when Jacuzzi saw the "Russo Family boss" who stepped into the room a minute later, his eyes went round with shock. The boss was so far from what anyone had expected that even Molsa was a little startled.

"Huh? ...What? I think I've seen you somewhere..."

Jacuzzi had seen the child about two months before, but the vivid memories of what had happened before and after that got in the way, and the details escaped him.

Ignoring Jacuzzi, the child bowed respectfully to Molsa, who was seated near the back of the room.

"Thank you for agreeing to meet with me, Mr. Martillo. I know my visit is a breach of etiquette."

The boy who stood in front of the door was very attractive and clearly still in his early teens.

"My name is Ricardo Russo. I'm in charge of the Russo Family."

Ricardo spoke in a way that didn't match his years, gazing at Molsa with straightforward eyes.

* * *

"...I see. My apologies. You threw me for a second there, but from the way you talk and the look in your eyes, I can tell this isn't your idea of a joke." After a slight pause, Molsa apologized briefly, then checked on something. "The Russo Family... I remember. It was in the news at the end of last year; I heard about it on the radio... I seem to recall that the current boss was a Mr. Placido Russo, though."

At the end of the previous year, wanted for a variety of crimes, Placido had vanished from Chicago. As if they'd been waiting for him to disappear, the surrounding syndicates had swarmed his rights and interests like sharks. Rumor had it that the Russos had lost all their territory in just a few weeks.

This was what had provoked Molsa's question, but Ricardo answered without hesitation. "My grandfather abandoned all his responsibilities and evaporated. He probably isn't among the living at this point. Even if he were, it wouldn't be possible for him to act as the family's head. My parents also passed away a few years ago, so I am the direct successor."

After impassively explaining his own position, Ricardo lowered his eyes slightly and went on in a rather self-deprecating way. "That said, the Russo Family would have to officially admit it, and the family itself has collapsed..."

"I see... I never met them directly, but I'll pray that your relatives rest in peace."

"...Thank you very much. Although the family has lost its shape, I am looking for a way to earn our keep for the sake of the handful of remaining members. I am also doing so in the knowledge that asking is a disgrace. Please understand that."

"That's very frank of you. Why did you come to us, though? If you're looking for work, you'd do better to try the Runorata Family."

Even when confronted with this natural question, Ricardo didn't hesitate.

"A big syndicate would grind us to dust, and that would be the end of it. However, while the Martillo Family is a small outfit, you've maintained your independence in New York. I hope to find the keys to rebuilding the Russo Family here."

"...You really are frank. Essentially, you plan to earn your keep and steal our know-how, but you don't intend to become members of our family?"

"Yes, as I said. You're welcome to treat us like any of your local juvenile delinquents. If you decide that the restoration of our family has become a problem... Well, we'll cross that bridge when we come to it."

Ricardo spoke in a way that sounded mature beyond his years, like he was a philosopher. Molsa couldn't help feeling sad about that.

"What an age we're living in, when young people like you have that look in your eyes. If you're going to be picking up work from us, we can't have you accepting death that easily."

Half of Molsa's remark was an admonition to Ricardo, who no longer seemed like a child at all—but the other half was an indication that he was willing to give the group work.

Ricardo nodded quietly and spoke slowly. "To be honest, I was prepared to be mocked the moment you saw me. If you thought this was a joke, then that would be that. Mr. Martillo, you've been kind enough to speak with me as an equal. That alone would be enough to make me grateful for our encounter."

"You give me too much credit. When you get to be my age, you stop being able to tell kids and adults apart, that's all. You're sure you're all right with us, though? The Gandors aren't much different. Keith Gandor's a wise man. I guarantee he won't look down on you because you're a child."

As a matter of fact, since the Camorra weren't what they were used to, Molsa thought the group would probably have an easier time under the Gandor Family, a fellow mafia outfit. That was why he'd checked with Ricardo, but the boy shook his head.

"...There's actually one more reason I chose your organization."

"Oh?"

"I only found this out the other day myself, but...my bodyguard says he has a friend in the Martillo Family."

As Ricardo spoke, he shot a glance behind him. Following his gaze, Molsa and Jacuzzi shifted their attention to the shape outside the door.

"Huh…?" Jacuzzi blurted out. He had a clear memory of the man who was smiling in the shadows of the corridor.

The man had red eyes and teeth like an orca. His clothes were the sort a nobleman might have worn in another century, and the combination made him look like an actual vampire.

He'd encountered this man in various places—the top floor of Mist Wall in New York, a restaurant in a corner of Chicago, the top of the Nebula building—and he could sum up his impression of him in a single word: *dangerous*.

"Hello, hello. I'm Christopher, Ricardo's good friend and subordinate."

"I didn't say you could talk." Ricardo shot him a cold glare and then apologized to Molsa. "I'm sorry. As you can see from his appearance, this man has no common sense, but I guarantee his utility in a fight."

"I see. When I caught a glimpse of him in the shadows outside the door, I thought I'd finally seen a ghost, at my age. That would have been concerning… Well, if he's human, that's a relief," Molsa joked, shrugging. Then he looked at Christopher, who truly was strange, and asked him a brief question. "So who's your friend?"

At that, with a smile one could have called innocent, Christopher cheerfully gave him a name. "Firo. Firo Prochainezo. He's a great friend, and a great benefactor. He taught me how to get along with Nature and also about human common sense!"

Huh? Firo? Jacuzzi thought. *Firo… The guy I'm about to go meet?*

The sudden mention of the name again confused him even further.

This enigmatic part-time job, where he was supposed to gamble.

The appearance of the Russo Family.

The fact that this Ricardo kid had become the family's boss somewhere along the way.

Christopher's entrance.

Thinking back over the various things that had happened in this brief interval, Jacuzzi started to shake so hard his teeth chattered.

Huh? That's weird.

When he'd stepped into this room, had he accidentally wandered into some sort of dream world? Of course, if it was a dream, it was definitely a nightmare.

All I wanted was to see if they'd do anything about the money, but I...

Was the act of earning money always so full of trouble?

Breaking into a cold sweat, he tried to organize the things he knew, but he couldn't make a single one of them fall in line.

Unaware of Jacuzzi's mental state, Molsa impassively moved the conversation forward. "Oho... Firo, huh? He knows more people than you'd figure."

The man who led the Martillo Family stroked his chin, seeming amused. Then, with a youthful smile, he addressed Ricardo and Christopher. "Perfect timing, though. In that case, I'll have you give Firo a hand as well."

Agh, agh, agh, agh, agh!

Wait just a minute. We'll be working with that Christopher guy? I—I mean, he...he shot people dead at the top of that building...

Oh, but he'd mellowed out in that restaurant in Chicago.

If I could talk it over with Tim...

A variety of information spun around in Jacuzzi's mind.

The sense that he was being dragged into deep trouble kept getting stronger. He considered simply bolting the second he got outside.

"Ronny," Molsa said.

"Yes?"

"Once we're done here, take Jacuzzi and these guys over to Firo's casino."

"Understood, sir." Ronny nodded, then glanced his way and smiled. When he saw that, Jacuzzi had no choice but to steel himself.

He was about to hurl himself headlong into trouble again.

The gamble had already begun.

Chapter 5 The Girl in Black Regrets Nothing

Meanwhile An apartment somewhere in New York

Will I be able to kill him?

A woman in a black dress was thinking dangerous things that didn't match her style.

However, a look at the worn knife in her hand made her thoughts seem tame by comparison.

The blade had been polished to a mirror shine, and the girl's eyes were reflected in it.

Chané Laforet asked her reflection a question.

Have I changed?

She was remembering her past.

She'd always given everything she had for the sake of her father, Huey Laforet. She'd done whatever he wanted, killing included. She'd thought she'd grown up according to his wishes—but perhaps she wasn't there yet.

She might not have satisfied him yet.

No, it was probably presumptuous to wish for that.

Humans couldn't live without the sun, but that didn't mean it loved them.

She mustn't wish for her father's love. Being his tool was enough.

When he used her and threw her away, as long as he said her name in that final moment, it would be enough.

That single act would vindicate her entire life.

If he didn't call her name—

Sad as it was, it would simply mean she hadn't been good enough for him.

She could never resent her father.

Once she was certain she hadn't lost the smallest fragment of that resolve, Chané thought to herself again.

I have to kill him—that man. That damnable man who declared he'd kill Father.

Ladd Russo… Can *I kill him?*

The fact that there was a little doubt in her heart made Chané gasp.

She stabbed her knife into the table, as if she were running it through her own heart.

The weapon sank into the wooden tabletop with the force of a hatchet. Its blade didn't chip at all. From the many marks on the table, it seemed likely the girl had done this over and over, whenever she was upset with herself.

Realizing the back of her neck was damp with sweat, she slowly looked up.

She was leaving the world of self-examination and returning to reality.

"……"

Wordlessly, Chané began to pace around the room.

Ordinarily, she lived with Jacuzzi and the others at the Genoard family's second residence. However, when she wanted to be alone, she often came to this cheap apartment. Even Jacuzzi's group didn't know where she went.

The place had originally been a hideout for the Lemures. She'd been surprised it was still usable now that the team had been wiped out. The fact that there hadn't been any notice from the landlord was unsettling, but for now, Chané was still using it as a hideaway.

It probably hadn't been built all that long ago. The color of the stone walls was new, and she didn't see any damage on the ceiling. Not only that, it had a comparatively new bathroom with a shower, the type that had grown popular in the 1920s.

Realizing even her palms were sweaty, Chané put her knife away and headed for that bathroom, her face still expressionless.

⇔

"......"

As a rule, Chané didn't use hot water when she showered.

Even as the frigid February water pelted her, she stayed lost in her own world, her expression unchanging.

She stood in a bathroom where no steam hung in the air, her beautiful limbs bare in the spray.

Instead of seeming erotic, her toned muscles and lithe body gave her the same sort of pure beauty as an ancient Greek statue.

"......"

While the cold water made her body tense, there was one boiling thought in her heart: She had to kill.

She was trying to summon the unshakable killer she once was.

To that end, first, she reflected on the change that had occurred in her from the perspective of her previous self.

I've lost my sharp edges.

How many years has it been since the last time I killed someone?

On the Flying Pussyfoot, she'd done away with the white-suited nobodies.

Now that she thought about it, that might have been a bad move.

Back then...I...

That wasn't for Father. I killed based on my own feelings.

As she'd walked through the train, she'd met a man who was trying to kill a young girl—a senator's daughter—whom the black-suited people intended to take hostage.

True, when she'd killed the man in the white suit before he could kill the girl, she'd been following the black suits' orders. However, the man had been about to kill the young girl to satisfy his own desires, and if someone had told her a very tiny bit—possibly less than one percent, but still—of her urge to end his life had been personal, she couldn't have denied it.

Her goal was to kill for the sake of her mission. If a speck of the sense that she wouldn't lose any sleep over killing a particular target mingled with the mission, did that make it a betrayal of her father?

In actual fact, she didn't think that one kill had changed her all that much. Although, if the leak of a single drop of water was how dam failures began, that might have been hers.

Immediately after that, she'd turned those violent feelings mixed with rage on Ladd Russo.

After, bemusement had joined the tangle inside her, and she had focused those emotions on the red monster.

Once she'd left the train, she'd turned a mixture of homicidal malice and confusion on a guy named Graham.

And after all of those experiences and so much time with no orders to follow, she'd gone several years without killing anyone.

Unfortunately, that man in the white suit, Ladd, wasn't the sort of soft enemy she'd be able to kill in a state like this.

Graham was devoted to Ladd. Depending on the situation, he might end up helping him.

A helper.

The moment she thought that, a man's face flickered through her mind—and her heart grew more unsettled than ever before.

"......"

She turned off the shower, and the spray stopped.

Countless water droplets trickled over Chané's skin, which was as smooth as polished marble.

Her expression was desolate.

She'd never show such melancholy in public.

She didn't know how her face looked right now, but she knew the identity of the complicated emotions that were welling up inside her. In her heart, she spoke his name.

...Claire.

I really have gone astray.

The moment she thought of the possibility that Graham would come to help, Chané had automatically remembered what the man had said to her.

"—Or should I kill the guy who's trying to kill your family? That white suit?"

He'd said it on the roof of a speeding train.

His words hadn't been lost in the rattle of the wheels against the tracks. They'd reached Chané's ears with startling clarity.

"So I had an idea: If I marry you, I'll be Huey's son. That'll make him family for me, too, and in that case, problem solved."

It had been an impossible proposal.

At the time, it had been hard for Chané to understand what he was saying.

She'd even wondered whether it might be some kind of code.

"Unlike your comrades, I won't sell you out.

"I'd never need to, see. Tough guys, people who are stronger than anyone, never betray their comrades. There's just no sense in it. And I'm strong. Understand?

"I also won't steal the secret of Huey's immortality, the way you're worried about. If he says he'll give it to me, sure, I'll take it, but I won't grab it away from him. I don't need to."

However, later on, Chané realized something—or rather, she was forced to see it.

The man was simply telling her what, for him, was the truth.

"Even without the power of immortality, there's no way I'm gonna die. Because I believe I won't. So you just stay quiet and believe in me.

"Believe that I'm a man who'll never die."

Even now, she could recall that red monster's words vividly.

She'd witnessed immeasurable strength, which was great enough to make what he'd said a reality here in New York, time and time again.

Claire Stanfield.

Now, he was calling himself Felix Walken, but Chané still called him Claire, even though no one else did.

Call wasn't quite the word for it: She was mute, so she simply thought of him by that name, in her heart.

For the most part, Claire had understood what she wanted to say just by looking into her eyes. Chané found this very strange, but she'd never thought it was creepy. On the contrary, the fact that her thoughts were getting through to someone made her feel the same emotion she felt when her father praised her: pure delight.

Chané wasn't incompetent enough to deny her own feelings by force.

After all, if she hadn't even been able to analyze herself, she'd never have been any use to Huey.

I feel...fond of Claire.

She could accept this as fact, and that made her sadder than anything. She didn't think Claire had softened her sharp edges personally, but in another sense, he'd defanged her.

I'm...hopeless...

I'm sure I'll end up relying *on Claire.*

After all, I trust him...

She felt no hesitation about killing her father's enemies, but she couldn't deny that she had lost her edge.

Even if she didn't win, Claire would handle it somehow. She understood better than anyone that she could not allow herself to be dependent. However, she couldn't completely banish that feeling from her heart.

After all, she knew Claire had an absolute strength, and she could trust him more than any of the *others* she'd met so far.

If Chané asked him to help with this, he was bound to say, *Sure. I'll kill him for you. You just take it easy, Chané.*

To Chané, there was a pain in this as well.

I can't do anything for Claire. If I rely on him, I won't be able to move—not even for Father's sake. If I'm no use to Father, I'm worthless.

I'm worthless, so why does Claire always...smile at me?

For a little while, there in the bathroom, Chané thought to herself with her eyes lowered.

She was thinking she really did have to kill Ladd Russo herself.

To reclaim the fangs she'd lost.

To face Claire as his equal.

And more than anything, she had to stay the version of herself that was useful to her father.

I have to think back—to the time when I wielded my blades without thinking of anything.

Yes... Just like that time...

She was remembering what had happened right before their assault on the train.

The man who'd sold her father out and tried to make the Lemures his personal property.

For a man who was only a little older than she was, maybe he'd shown impressive initiative, but the only thing that half-formed resourcefulness and recklessness had gotten him was a miserable death.

When she'd cut off his right hand at the wrist, Chané hadn't felt anything to speak of. She hadn't even felt anger over his betrayal of her father. It had been like crumpling a piece of scrap paper.

Now, as she looked back, an emotion that wasn't anger welled up.

It was genuine pity. How unlucky and foolish that man had been, getting above himself and racing toward his own death.

Right now, though, she didn't need that pity, either.

Chané simply looked back on the past to retake what she'd felt at the time.

His face was hazy, but she remembered his name clearly.

Nader.

Nader Schasschule.

That was the name of the last man Chané had cut down while feeling absolutely nothing.

She hadn't killed him directly, but Goose had blown up their hideout immediately afterward, so he probably wasn't among the living.

Whether he'd died in the explosion or bled to death, she'd set him up to die.

Like a clockwork machine, with no emotion whatsoever, she'd simply performed the job she'd been given. He hadn't been enough of an opponent for her to feel anger toward him. She'd simply been taking out the trash. She'd cut off his hand without even feeling pity. She had to remember what that had been like.

The sensation of her knife sinking into flesh, Nader's expression as all the hope drained out of it. Her own heart, unwavering even as she was splashed with the traitor's fresh blood.

After silently immersing herself in that memory for a few seconds and quietly regulating her breathing, she raised her head.

Her face was perfectly blank. She could no longer feel the faintest trace of the weakness that had been there a moment ago.

It was just like before, when she'd been a machine who wielded her knives for her father's sake.

Still expressionless, Chané dried herself off with a white towel.

She'd heard that Ladd Russo would be back tonight at the earliest.

She'd settle her score with him then. She wouldn't let him take the initiative.

Chané didn't want to cause trouble for Jacuzzi and the others, so she resolved to act on her own, without returning to the Genoard family's mansion.

Just as she'd made that decision, her sharp, focused senses caught the faint creak of a floorboard.

—!

The sound had come from outside the bathroom, probably from the bedroom.

It had been so quiet that she would ordinarily have missed it.

Chané didn't remember hearing the door open or close, but she was certain.

Somebody's here.

The only one who knew she was using this apartment was Claire Stanfield. Nonetheless, he wouldn't have opened the door stealthily, and if he'd heard that she was in the shower, he'd immediately have said, *Okay if I peep?*

Quietly narrowing her eyes and holding her breath, Chané picked up the knife she'd left beside the sink. Even though keeping one in the bathroom would risk the tool rusting, she'd chosen to keep it within arm's reach, a choice she was glad of now.

She slowly opened the bathroom door. She could see the bedroom at the end of the hall.

The intruder seemed to be standing in a blind spot beyond the doorway; she couldn't see him from the hallway. However, there was definitely a shadow moving on the floor of that room.

Calculating where the intruder would be standing from the window and the position of that shadow, Chané erased all emotion from every cell in her body.

It was probably best to assume this wasn't a thief who'd just happened to break in. If anyone knew about this apartment, it would probably be one of the former Lemures.

Spike.

The name of the sniper who'd been her colleague came to mind. On the other hand, she couldn't see a sniper deciding to come to a cramped place like this, where he'd be at a disadvantage. In that case, was it his companion, the former Felix?

Either way, she couldn't afford to get careless or hold back. She also didn't need to; if that shadow belonged to Claire, he'd probably stop her knife easily.

Coming to that conclusion, Chané jumped as noiselessly as a cat and reached the door in a single leap. She didn't wait for her opponent to hear her land and turn around as she made her next move.

From a low stance, Chané unleashed a low-trajectory uppercut.

The hilt of the sharp knife was in her fist—she'd sink its blade into her opponent's neck.

That was all she had to do.

Without hatred or regret.

She just had to accept the fact that she'd killed her opponent.

That alone would be enough to solidly return her to the past.

However—

Just before the blade reached the intruder, Chané froze up.

It wasn't just a physical response.

……*?*

……

……—

"———*?!*"

Her heart passed through several stages of emotion before it went completely blank.

Incidentally, the man's clothes, which were reflected in her eyes, were so very, very white—and they made his glossy black hair stand out in even sharper contrast.

"Why don't you at least put on some clothes?"

The moment she heard that voice, Chané thought she must be dreaming. When had it begun? Had she thought so deeply in the shower that she'd fallen asleep? Or was she still on the Flying Pussyfoot, and had all the rest been a dream, including her encounter with Claire?

As that worry began to spiral, the man's voice pulled her back to reality.

"People will think you're an immodest child, Chané."

Chané's naked body was as well-proportioned as a model's, but even when the man looked at it, he didn't blush. He wore the same smile he'd worn as he watched her grow up, from the time she was very young.

It was more the smile of an artisan gazing at his creation than that of a father looking at his daughter.

And it was that rather cold smile that convinced her.

The one who was standing in front of her was, without a doubt, him.

Her father.

The immortal by the name of Huey Laforet. The terrorist who was trying to transform the world.

Surprise over several things—including the fact that one of his eyes was covered by a bandage—crashed over Chané's heart like a furious wave. However, at the same time, endless joy coursed through her, telling her none of her questions mattered at all.

"......!......!"

As his daughter stood stunned, her eyes brimming with all sorts of emotions, Huey simply and blandly stated his business.

"I need a few assistants. I've a new experiment to run." The man spoke in a leisurely way—certainly not like someone who was talking to his own daughter. "Will you help me, Chané?"

There was no reason for her to turn him down.

She wouldn't even have minded risking her life.

If Huey had said *I want your heart* at this point, she would immediately have plunged her knife into her own breast.

Chané's eyes were filled with delight and a will that was stronger than it had ever been.

"There's no need for all that enthusiasm, Chané." The man smiled at her, shaking his head.

"After all, this experiment is a bit of a gamble."

⇔

Meanwhile On the Atlantic Ocean

"It sounds as though Master Huey has made it safely into Manhattan, the site of the experiment."

"He's early."

It was February, and a cold wind blustered over the Atlantic.

The men were conversing while they stood on the deck of a large cargo ship. They were clad in gas masks and black cold-weather gear from head to toe. They couldn't see each other's faces at all.

"Yes, he said he wanted to speak with his daughter first."

"...That's unusual. Leeza's one thing, but to think he'd go see Chané voluntarily..."

"He may be planning to use every pawn at his disposal."

The man did seem to respect Huey. However, he clearly did not feel the same about Huey's daughter.

Standing by the ship's gunwale, the men went on talking with tension in their voices.

"Since the Lemures are gone, I'd guessed he'd come to Larva, and to us in Rhythm, but..."

"Didn't think even Time would be out in full force."

These men, members of Rhythm, were looking at several shapes floating on the sunset ocean.

The shapes were *several dozen seaplanes and five flying boats.*

It had been a little over thirty years since the Wright brothers made the first successful flight in 1903.

Since that time, aircraft had undergone remarkable developments. The Great War had generated a demand for military planes, and they were continuing to evolve on a variety of fronts. In the midst of this, seaplanes and flying boats—both of which could take off and land on water—had been developing as well and were spreading around the world.

They would later lose their share to landplanes. However, takeoffs on short runways were still a strain for the technology of this era, and since oceans and rivers could be used as long runways, seaplanes were considered extremely useful. Some models from outstanding manufacturers could achieve speeds of over four hundred forty miles per hour, and it truly was the golden age of seaplanes.

The men from Rhythm were looking at the stars of the aviation world. On top of that, while they were based on planes from existing manufacturers, they seemed to have been tinkered with here and there. That said, it wasn't yet possible to tell specifically how they'd been modified.

At that time, seaplanes weren't built with attached machine guns. For the most part, they were used for patrols, recon, and surveys of ballistic impacts. With this many of them, though, if explosives were dropped from the air by hand, they could function quite well as weapons.

As a matter of fact, only an airline company or the military could have procured this many aircraft.

Naturally, Huey was neither of these things.

This overwhelming equipment sent a chill down the spines of the two Rhythm members.

"Is the upcoming experiment a war?" he asked, his tone completely serious.

The other man shook his head. "According to Master Huey, it's a modest gamble."

"...Has he ever done anything that wasn't a gamble?"

"Right, so it's business as usual. Master Huey's experiments are always gambles, and he probably just wants to know what will happen.

"This time, he's raised the stakes a bit, that's all."

Chapter 6 There's No Other Way to Live

On the highway In a passenger car

"Oho... So Uncle Placido finally made himself scarce, huh?"

"All their territory has been taken by other syndicates already...," Lua replied.

Ladd burst out laughing. "Ha! I told him so! It's just like I said: Uncle was all washed up. Actually, I'm impressed he hung on for three years... Maybe nobody knows where he went, but my money's on somewhere six feet under." After summarily predicting his uncle's death, Ladd, in the backseat, spoke to the man who was riding shotgun. "You're a lucky guy, Nader. She says Uncle Placido's not around anymore. Well, back when they went and locked Lua up, it was already a sure thing that I was gonna crush the family."

"Y-yeah... You're right."

Rocked by the motion of the car, with those dangerous words in his ears, Nader Schasschule thought, *Where did I go wrong?*

He looked back over his life. Where had the fork in the road been?

Nader had joined the Lemures just after he turned sixteen.

For several years before that, he'd lived by running cheap, childish flimflams.

He'd run away from his rural home, had gotten through all sorts of trouble using nothing more than his glib tongue, and had made a habit of ingratiating himself with powerful people. In the time it took him to grow from the ringleader of the local kids to a minor mafia executive, he lived off strong people one after another, like a hermit crab going through shells.

As he did so, Nader's own attitude gradually grew bigger. He could feel power at his fingertips.

There's a proverb about a fox that borrows a tiger's authority, and when it came to finding an even stronger tiger, you could have said Nader was twice as greedy as the average person. As a matter of fact, he might have had a gift for it. He'd borrowed the authority of a whole parade of tigers. When one tiger was near death, he'd skin it and offer its pelt to the next one. In other words, he was an opportunistic small-timer, but you could say that his nose for power was the real deal.

At last, he'd made a fatal mistake: The final tiger whose authority he'd borrowed had been Huey Laforet.

Once he'd infiltrated the Lemures, he'd tried to find out just what kind of person their leader was—and after one look at him, he knew this Huey guy wasn't a tiger or anything like it. He was something far more dire. The man's authority was poison. Once Nader borrowed it, he'd be finished. His own skin just might rot off.

He harbored a vague fear of Huey.

He had his doubts about the man's immortality, but he was certain Huey was a bad person.

He didn't see us as his subordinates or companions or anything like that.

Tools... No, that ain't right, either.

It was like he didn't care if we broke. He had the eyes of a kid watching ants drown.

Feeling a chill run down his spine, Nader cut his memories of Huey short.

It's his fault my life went off the rails.

After Nader joined the Lemures, he'd made a very bad decision.

Since he'd developed an indefinable fear of Huey, Nader avoided ingratiating himself with him directly. Instead, he waited for his chance as the flunky of a man named Goose. One day, an opportunity arrived: Huey got nabbed by the Bureau of Investigation.

His nose for danger wasn't fully working yet, and Nader ignored his instincts. He made contact with his next tiger—Placido Russo—and got to work poaching the better part of the Lemures.

However, the price for not trusting his intuition had been far too great. He'd lost his right hand, nearly died, and ended up on the run from the Russo Family.

He'd been betrayed, not by his search for new power, but by his fear of Huey. That had probably been the decisive difference between all his other moves and this one.

Should I have just kept on listening to that asshole Goose? No... That's not right, either. I dunno what was up, but even without me ratting them out, those guys were practically falling apart already. I don't know what happened on that train, but if I'd been on board...

He couldn't visualize himself surviving that carnage, and he ground his teeth quietly.

Maybe things had started going off the rails for him when he joined the Lemures, or possibly when he got involved with Huey in the first place.

Where had the gears slipped? He thought about it again, but the answer wouldn't come. The more he thought, the further back he went. He wasn't enough of a pessimist to think his very birth had been a mistake, but... Before long, he registered the most important junction, the one an ordinary person would probably have thought of first.

Why did I become a con artist in the first place?

If he'd taken the wrong path, could it have started there?

By any form of normal logic, entering underworld society by choice was a mistake.

Nader was reluctant to admit that, though.

I just wanted power, that's all.

He hadn't cared whether he came by it honestly or through underworld society. He'd simply wanted the strength to do everything his way. He'd thought that if he borrowed others' authority, skinned them, and kept wearing those skins, someday he'd manage to acquire real power. As a matter of fact, if he'd managed to successfully sell out the Lemures, he'd pictured himself ultimately taking over the Russo Family.

But I screwed up.

I managed to get even with Goose, but in the end, I'm just a pitiful traitor.

Come to think of it...I ran into a real head case in front of the station in Chicago that day.

I forgot his name, but...I can't believe what he managed to do even though he was weak.

All to save scum like me.

Nader came very close to basking in a certain memory, but at the same time, he remembered something.

Oh, that's right. That was it.

Memories of a distant day rose in his mind.

I wanted to get stronger and become a hero.

It was a childish promise he'd made when he was twelve or so, to a neighborhood girl who was about five years younger.

When I grow up, I'm gonna be a hero!
Yeah, like Wyatt Earp or Jesse James!
Just you watch—I'll get super strong!
And then, hey... I could protect you, too, if you want.

His own words from when he was a kid echoed in his mind.

He had lied. The girl had been like a little sister to him, and he had been showing off for her. Still, he remembered the girl had smiled happily back at him.

I was a total idiot. I said I'd become a hero, and then I turn out like this?

Come to think of it, I wonder what she's doing now.

Remembering his younger childhood friend, Nader had a sudden thought.

After he'd gotten his revenge on Goose and was free of the Lemures, he'd planned to go back to his hometown and work his dad's cornfields. When he got there, though, that girl wasn't in town anymore.

It made him a little sad, but he was relieved she wouldn't see what a loser he was now.

Putting it behind him, he tried to get the "power" to throw away his past self and live a new life.

That way, one day, when the girl came back to town, he'd be able to give her a genuine smile.

However, he'd been forced to see something—he was still underestimating Huey Laforet.

Right after Nader got back, the cornfields he'd inherited from his father *burned to ashes, barn and all.* Stunned, he'd walked back into his room at the house where he'd grown up, and there, he found a note on his bed.

Why don't you tremble in your shoes like the traitor you are?
—Hilton

He could see the spite in the handwriting, and the moment he saw it, his vision had gone black.

He'd heard the name "Hilton" before. She was a liaison that Goose contacted from time to time. Every time they met, she'd looked different, but she'd probably been in disguise. Either that, or it was an alias that multiple women used.

Realizing he was being watched—and targeted—Nader got out of the house, fast, and rushed to the town's main street. It was the most densely populated place around. Once he'd confirmed the people coming and going around him were all perfectly ordinary residents, he started to breathe a sigh of relief.

"Say, mister?"

At his feet, a small girl looked up at him, smiling.

She didn't look like she was ten years old yet. She reminded him a bit of his childhood friend, and Nader gave a small smile and patted her head. "What, little lady?" He spoke in a kind voice that wasn't at all like him, possibly due to his relief, but the very next instant—

—the smile vanished from the girl's face, and her voice filled with icy hatred.

* * *

"...Do you actually think you can get away, Nader Schasschule?"

After that, his memories were hazy. He didn't remember where he'd run to, or how, or whether even more frightening things had happened to him when he got there. The next thing he knew, he was banging on the door of the Bureau of Investigation office and begging, "Some crazy bird's got me on her kill list. Please, lock me up!"

It had been three years since then—and here he was.

Frankly, he was terrified. He had no idea when the Russo Family or Hilton might take a shot at him. For that reason, the fact that he was getting a ride from this Ladd guy was technically a good thing, but...

On the other hand, I've got a strong hunch that I've stepped into a very nasty mess.

The incident a little while ago had clearly shown him just how dangerous Ladd was. It was also obvious that the guy was more of a mad dog than a tiger, and it wasn't going to be possible to borrow his authority.

If I stick around, I bet he'll drag me into an even bigger mess.

I have to split up with him somehow...

After that earlier trouble, the guy still hadn't grilled him about his connection to the Flying Pussyfoot. Nader had the feeling that telling Ladd about it wouldn't end up working against him. However, the very fact that Ladd had taken an interest in him might.

In the end, Nader had already rolled the dice. He even suspected that this situation, where disaster followed disaster to his door, was the result of that one choice. He'd calmed his heart down by telling himself that there was no other way for him to live at this point.

Even if that was just a *cheat.*

With a little sigh, Nader started listening to the conversation in the car, hoping to find a way out.

"So yours truly is the only survivor of the Russo Family, huh? Kinda lonely."

"Young Master Ricardo's still around," the young man in the driver's seat told Ladd.

"Ah. Ricardo, huh? Ricardo. Yeah. That takes me back. Him, too—he's still a kid, but he's like a damn philosopher. Acts like he could die whenever and not give a damn. Ah, I can't explain it. He's like Lua, but not."

Ladd sounded bored. The woman sitting next to him asked, "Did Ricardo start acting that way…after the incident…?"

"Yeah, when my cuz and his wife got blown to kingdom come. Car bomb," Ladd answered.

Goddammit. The conversation just keeps getting uglier.

The impulse to drop his head into his hands crashed over Nader, but he curbed it and sat quietly in the passenger seat. Beside him, the driver—a guy named Shaft—spoke up as if he'd just remembered something relevant. "Oh, speaking of young Master Ricardo, I hear he's in New York right now. It sounds like he's planning to work under some other gang and rebuild the Russo Family… I mean, it's just a rumor, so I don't really know the details."

"Rebuild the Russos? That kid?" At that unexpected bit of news, Ladd looked mildly surprised. "Oho. I'll be looking forward to that. That gives me more to do in the ol' Big Apple."

Ladd crossed his arms cheerfully and leaned back in his seat. Just then, a rapping noise sounded beside him. When he looked over, Graham's upside-down face was peeking in through the window. So that Lua and Ladd could be alone together in the backseat, he'd considerately gotten on top of the car instead.

He was riding on the roof of a car that was going relatively fast, which meant it wasn't the sort of act that the word *consideration* was typically used for, but Nader was determined not to get involved with these people, so he didn't point that out.

Graham was lying flat on his stomach up there, and when Ladd rolled down the window for him, he peeked in. "So hey, Ladd. There's this huge convoy of cars coming up behind us. Think they're chasing us?"

"Hmm?" Ladd turned around and saw a procession of luxury

cars approaching from the rear. "Nah… They don't look like they're chasing anybody."

The road was a broad one, so Shaft checked the rearview mirror, pulled the car over toward the shoulder, and kept driving. At that, eight high-end cars passed them, followed by one large truck. Two motorbikes brought up the rear, and they could make out the fact that the men on both bikes were identical to each other. It looked almost like a military parade. The expensive cars stayed the exact same distance from one another as they drove, exerting an intense feeling of pressure on their surroundings. The pair of motorcycle riders in the rear almost seemed to be guarding the big truck, and the odd combination gave Ladd's heart a thrill. "Whoa, whoa, whoa. What the hell is that? Think it's a circus or something? Bit too ritzy for that, though… Getting a whole group of rich folks together and putting 'em on the flying trapeze and making 'em fight lions—that sounds pretty entertaining, don't it?"

"Don't say stuff like that, all right?" Shaft said. "…That's the Runorata Family."

That remark made Ladd's eyes shine. This close encounter with the Runorata Family, one of the biggest syndicates of the area, seemed to have made the emotions welling up in his heart impossible to control. "The Runorata Family, huh? I like the sound of that. Let's pick a fight with 'em—c'mon, let's do it! Stomp on the accelerator and ram 'em, Shaft!"

"No way! I don't want to die yet!"

"Hey, c'mon. Not wanting to die is a good thing, but you gotta get in on the party, or you'll lose out. I mean, you might lose big even if you do get in on it, but still."

"I'm surprised you can say that when Lua's with you."

Shaft's commonsense retort made Nader feel just a little kinship with him. Meanwhile, Lua was murmuring "Die…here…with Ladd" and blushing, while Ladd and Graham were seriously discussing whether or not to attack the Runorata Family. Watching them made him feel like he should have never gotten into this car.

Either way, what I want right now is information.

Once the conversation settled down, he turned to Shaft in the hopes of getting some of that information. "Those cars… They looked like they were going our way. Is the Runorata Family based in New York?"

However, Shaft answered in the negative. "No. They're mostly in New Jersey. Oh… I wonder if it has to do with that one thing."

That remark had seemed to imply something more, so Nader pressed him. "What one thing?"

It must not have been a secret or anything, because Shaft flatly replied, "The hotel."

"Hotel?"

"They built a huge hotel in New York, just recently. From what I hear, they're opening a restaurant that takes up an entire basement floor."

"Huh."

"And the thing is, the owner of that restaurant is a member of the Runorata Family."

It didn't seem to be a particularly unusual story. Thinking this probably wouldn't have anything to do with him, Nader felt relieved—and then that relief was destroyed as Shaft continued with more dangerous news.

"That said, they broke into an area where major outfits are fighting over territory. They've made a lot of enemies, so they probably need an escort that big."

"……"

"One floor below that restaurant, they've made a big ol' casino, although they're calling it the 'spare guest rooms'… Or that's the rumor anyway."

Shaft went on with his explanation, impassively. Nader wasn't sure how to respond.

As if to say he didn't care about that answer, Ladd broke in from the rear seat. "A casino? Hey, nice! Those places attract morons who think their luck is great and don't have the slightest doubt that they're gonna live forever! I bet they'd be worth killing!"

"Uh, do you think you could avoid the k-word for a bit? You're scaring Mr. Nader."

"Oh yeah? Sorry 'bout that, Nader! I'll pay you back for this favor someday. Assuming I remember."

I don't care if you forget, just lemme out already.

Nader was about to start crying on the inside. However, his wishes would not be granted as Ladd went on giving vent to his own curiosity.

"Come to think of it, Firo said something about being a casino owner, too."

"...An owner?"

"Nah, not an owner. Maybe a manager? Well, whatever. Okay... Once we get to NYC, let's hunt down that casino first thing. We'll go big, stake all our assets, and test our luck! Sound good, Nader?!"

Huh? I'm already locked into this bet, too?

It was a perfectly natural question, and he almost asked it, but he ultimately wasn't able to stand up to Ladd's presence.

And so the small-timer got closer and closer to New York.

He had no idea what results his dice roll would yield or what payoff might be waiting for him.

Chapter 7 The Rival Isn't Stupid

Somewhere in New York A major street

"Ngh… I wonder if the other guys are worried. I did give them a call, but…"

As Jacuzzi trudged along with tears in his eyes, Rail casually teased him. "Get it together, Jacuzzi. When you work under the table, aren't you all washed up if people underestimate you?"

"If being underestimated is all it takes to keep everybody safe, I'll let them underestimate us all day."

"You're pretty wishy-washy, huh? Don't you have any pride?"

Up until a moment ago, Rail had been crying, but by the time Jacuzzi had rejoined her, she'd been her usual self again.

However, when a voice spoke behind them, her expression instantly went stiff and awkward.

"There's nothing wrong with that, Rail. Sometimes you'll get licked, and knowing how to endure it is important."

"You can talk like that because you don't know Jacuzzi, Chris."

Ultimately, it had been decided that they'd go to Firo Prochainezo's gambling den, and they were all following Ronny at a slight distance. Parenthetically, Isaac and Miria were still at the restaurant. They were probably asking Molsa for jobs of their own right about now. Jacuzzi had an extreme fear of Ronny, but Rail, who didn't know the reason behind that fear, had written him off as a genuine coward.

With regard to Jacuzzi's treatment, Ricardo had bluntly told him, "The Russo Family isn't your enemy any longer. After all, even if we went after you, we don't have the power to keep you from taking us out instead." Then he'd added, "If you want me to take responsibility for what my grandfather did, I'd like to have that discussion another time."

Jacuzzi had shaken his head emphatically and said, "N-no… Your grandpa was the one we had a grudge against," and they'd ended up reconciling.

S-still, I wonder what'll happen with Ladd Russo.

I never found the opportunity to bring it up, but we'll have to do something about him, too…

If he spoke to him properly, through Ricardo, they might be able to settle things peacefully. If a kid like Ricardo approached them humbly, even Jack probably wouldn't insist on getting his way.

On that thought, Jacuzzi examined his remaining worries.

That aside, I wonder why that red-eyed man is here…?

Whether or not he knew what Jacuzzi was thinking, Christopher cackled. "No, I mean it, it's actually amazing: Did you know that, ages back, there was a torture where they'd have rats lick your stomach?"

At the word *torture*, Jacuzzi had steeled himself, but when he heard the rest of the sentence, he felt relieved. "I—I might be able to last through that, somehow… I bet it would really tickle, though."

"See, first, they'd put lots of rats in an iron pot, then use the person's belly as the lid. Their belly would be covered with honey or saltwater—I forget what, but anyway, it was something rats probably like."

"S-stop, please… Just listening to that is making me ticklish." Jacuzzi's face went pale as he imagined the scene.

Christopher ignored him. "Nah, don't worry. You won't feel that way for long."

"?" Jacuzzi tilted his head.

"They'd put that person on their back so that the pot was upside down. Then they'd put hot rocks or something on the base of the pot and presto—as they tried to get away from the heat, the swarm of rats would start digging into that soft, flesh-colored soil…"

"Yaaaaaaaaugh!" Imagining it vividly, Jacuzzi screamed.

"Burning rats? That's cruel."

"Not that part! That wasn't the important part, Rail!"

"I'm joking. Seriously, Jacuzzi, you're really easy to mess with."

Jacuzzi had teared up again, and Rail laughed at him. Every so often, she'd sneak a glance at Christopher, then quickly look away.

Ricardo sighed. "If you want, you can come to the apartment we're renting tonight."

Rail gave Ricardo a contemptuous smile. "Ha-ha! Well, aren't you considerate? Don't be a creep. And anyway, what was that stuff you said? Do you seriously think you can rebuild the Russo Family? A weak little girl like you!"

Rail's dislike for Ricardo was based in their similarities, *including the fact that they were both women who were keeping it a secret.* She braced herself, wondering how Ricardo would react, but…

The girl seemed to be brooding; she hadn't heard what Rail had said.

Thinking this was odd, Christopher asked, "What's up, Ricardo?"

"It might be better if…we didn't go to that casino today…" Ricardo murmured the words almost as if she were talking to herself.

Christopher was perplexed. For that matter, so were Rail and Jacuzzi. Up until now, Ricardo had been all for going, and they had to know why she'd suddenly changed her mind. Ricardo looked down for a moment, still expressionless, then sighed.

"…No, never mind. It might actually be wiser to *get this over with quickly.*"

⇔

A lone shadow trailed Jacuzzi's group, unobtrusively.

It was Ennis, who'd just finished helping out at Alveare. She was concerned not only about what Rail had said to her but also by Christopher's very existence, so she'd followed them. Hearing that they were headed for Firo's gambling den had reminded her of the incident at Mist Wall. She was worried that Christopher might go on a rampage.

This kind of work was not new to Ennis. As Szilard's underling, she'd shadowed people and conducted infiltrations many times. Except for her unusual suit, she'd completely melted into the crowd.

Or at least she thought she had.

"What are you doing, Ennis?" a young voice said from behind her.

When she turned, the immortal boy who'd been living with her for the past few years was standing there.

"...Czes."

"Why are you tailing those people? Is it for work?"

"No, that isn't it..."

Ennis wasn't sure how to explain, but Czes went on without waiting. "Not only that, but *both of you at once...*"

Huh?

Wondering what he meant by "both," she looked around, and—

A girl poked her head out from behind a truck with a canvas-covered bed that was parked by the side of the road. It was Annie, who'd started working as a waitress at Alveare last year.

"Eh-heh-heh! You caught me." The other girl was unapologetic.

Ennis called to her. "Annie? Why are you...?"

"I just happened to see you, Ennis, and you seemed a little odd, so I followed you. If you were watching somebody else, then we made a train!"

Watching Jacuzzi's retreating group out of the corner of her eye, Ennis apologized. "I'm sorry. I didn't mean to cause trouble for you or worry you..."

Annie asked her a pointed question. "The place where Firo works is that way, isn't it?"

"Y-yes..."

I mustn't get her involved in this. Ennis averted her eyes and fell silent, but she was completely unprepared for Annie's next question.

"By the way, Ennis... What do you think of Firo?"

When he heard that question, Czes thought *Aha...* and smiled inwardly.

This waitress had been a little odd for the past month—specifically, since Firo had gotten back from prison. She kept stealing glances at him, and although the two of them had hardly spoken at all before, she'd begun going out of her way to talk to him. Firo always seemed to politely brush her off, but she kept talking to him as if this was all she needed. The Martillo Family members who were constantly at Alveare had been gossiping about Annie: *Do you think she maybe...?* Hearing that just now had convinced Czes.

Firo's a pretty smooth operator, huh, he thought, unconcerned.

However, Czes didn't know something about Annie.

She had two other names.

Her other faces were peculiar ones: Hilton, a liaison who reported directly to Huey, and Leeza, Huey's biological daughter.

Meanwhile, Ennis responded, perplexed: "...Ah? He's family..."

Why would Annie ask that question now?

Ennis didn't know what Annie really was, and she was largely oblivious to romantic matters to begin with, so she decided Annie was simply being weird.

"Family, hmm? That's nice. Family."

It wasn't clear what Annie had thought of Ennis's answer. She gave a thin smile.

Looking between her and the confused Ennis, Czes murmured, "This is getting interesting," in a voice quiet enough for no one else to hear.

After all, he didn't know about either Hilton or Leeza. He just assumed that a young female employee had fallen for Firo and arbitrarily decided that Ennis, who hadn't even noticed her own feelings, was her rival.

Granted, although the situation was a bit more convoluted, he was basically correct.

⇔

Manhattan Little Italy

"*...No, never mind. It might actually be wiser to* get this over with quickly."

Don't even joke about that. Quick or not, this is bad news coming out of nowhere.

When he heard Ricardo's voice in his head, Shaft—who was one of Sham's bodies—muttered to himself silently, breaking out in a cold sweat.

"Sham" was a system Huey had created—an entity that used one mind to run multiple bodies, just as abnormal as the immortals. He took over the bodies of people who drank a special liquid and made them part of himself. There was a theory that the liquid itself was Sham's true form—but even Sham didn't know whether that was true.

Due to a variety of circumstances, Ricardo hadn't actually had her mind taken over by Sham. She simply shared his knowledge and sometimes teamed up with him.

This won't be like that one restaurant, Ricardo!

Unfortunately, Ladd Russo, who was in the backseat of this car, was bound for Firo's underground casino.

If no one did anything, Graham and Christopher, who loathed each other, would meet, and Jacuzzi would come face-to-face with Ladd.

While the Martillo Family was small, the organization had clout. Shaft was a thug, but even Sham could tell if they tore up a casino run by a group that was home to the likes of Maiza and Firo, they would be inviting all kinds of hardship.

There's no benefit in making them take each other out at this stage!

At that restaurant in Chicago, he and Ricardo had conspired to have Graham and Christopher run into each other in order to get the situation moving. However, this wasn't the time to carelessly set the situation in motion.

With Mr. Huey and Victor's group in town, too, it'll just make the mess bigger!

Without betraying so much as a hint of this internal conflict, Shaft silently kept on driving. He'd considered buying time by pretending not to know where Firo's casino was and saying he needed to check into it, but maddeningly, Graham claimed he knew the way.

"To get to the Martillo Family casino, you hang a right up there, Shaft."

Graham was peeking into the driver's seat from up on the roof and navigating for him. Shaft glared at him in disgust. "Hey, why do you know where the casino is anyway, Mr. Graham?"

"Oh, I figured someday when my money ran out, I'd strike it rich."

"Are you good at gambling?" Shaft sounded dubious.

"No, I mean I'd strike the head of the guy who was transporting their takings..."

"You are so worthless!" Shaft yelled. "Argh, for Pete's sake, come to think of it, you *were* that kind of guy, weren't you, Mr. Graham?! Did you already forget how Nicola from the Gandors flattened you for trying that earlier?! He's got the biggest heart I've ever seen, so he wrote it off as delinquents playing a prank, but still! If he hadn't done that, we'd be feeding the fishes on the bottom of the Hudson right about now!"

That drew a response from Ladd in the backseat. "...Hunh? Kid Graham lost? In a fight?"

"Uh... Well... There's this fella in the Gandor Family, Nicola; he's a hell of a fighter. Graham went back for rematches lots of times, but he always got his ass handed to him..."

Up on the roof, they heard Graham launch into a long speech. "Hey, I won one and lost six. You forgot I won once. Shaft, you wouldn't happen to be a Martian wearing Shaft's skin, would you?"

Ladd might not have been listening to any of that, though. His lips twisted into a truly delighted smile. "Well, whaddaya know. It really is a big world. I should've partied a little harder last time I came to New York."

He lightly smacked a fist into his palm. As Shaft glanced at Ladd, he felt even more certain that now wasn't the time to let him run into Jacuzzi or Christopher.

Forced to ignore his resolution, though, Shaft still pulled the car over outside of Firo's casino.

It would probably be a little longer before Jacuzzi and Christopher got there. He had to get Ladd and Graham to go elsewhere somehow.

Shaft fished up a certain piece of information from Sham's vast pool of knowledge and put it to work.

"Who… Right, Mr. Who!"

"Hunh?" Abruptly hearing the nickname of his childhood pal, Ladd frowned and looked at Shaft.

"N-no, I mean, once we meet this Firo guy, we may get tied up for a while, so wouldn't it be better to go see Who first?"

"Uh… Hold the phone, Who's in New York?"

"Yeah, I happened to see him the other day and thought, 'Huh! Isn't that Mr. Ladd's old friend?'"

That seemed to put Ladd in a great mood. He laughed with genuine amusement.

"Oho-hoooo! I see, how 'bout that! So that lug Who didn't get his ticket punched on the train, huh?! Well, he always was good at keeping himself outta trouble."

If he was actually good at staying out of trouble, he probably wouldn't have kept in touch with Ladd. Nader actually thought this at the same time Shaft did, but naturally, neither of them said it aloud.

"The thing is, Who's working as an assistant at a clinic that's just up the road a bit. With the car, we could get there in no time. Want to go say hello before we get settled in at the casino?"

"That's an idea… Yeah, maybe I should," Ladd said.

At that, Shaft mentally heaved a sigh of relief.

But then Ladd took a thick wad of bills from his wallet, which Lua had kept for him while he was in prison, and said, "All right, Nader. You go on in and get the roulette wheel warmed up for us." He tossed over the money.

"Wha—? Wait, what…?! Why?!"

"Well, watching me meet my old friend again would be boring for you, yeah?"

"I—I mean, yeah, but… But what's this money for?!"

As he looked at Nader, who was royally confused, Shaft also seemed to be thinking, *Quit making things more complicated!*

"I'm giving you that money, so go bet big. Get ready to blow it all. Hit the jackpot or lose your shirt, it don't matter—just make like a high roller. I wonder what Firo's gonna think when he finds out I'm your sponsor. Ha!"

"...You don't think I might just take this money and fade?"

"You're gonna run off with it? Hey, that's fine. If you do, it'll just mean I lost my bet."

When he heard that, Nader was convinced—Ladd really wasn't normal. He was a hedonist who lived for the moment.

For that very reason, Nader was scared. He couldn't help thinking that Ladd had omitted the part where he said, *Next time I see your mug, I'll just slaughter you, that's all.*

As a matter of fact, even if he did make off with the money, Ladd probably wouldn't think anything of it. Not that it mattered. *Even if he didn't think anything of it*, he'd probably throw lead at him anyway.

"Oh, but if you're planning to run, I want to hear about your connection to the Flying Pussyfoot incident before you take off... Well, if it happens, it happens. If you run, I'll give up."

Ladd never killed anyone he'd decided was his pal.

Nader didn't know about that rule, and he interpreted the remark to mean, "If you run, I'll give up on getting the story and kill you as soon as I find you." He was scared, but he clenched the wad of bills in his hand.

"...Okay if I keep my winnings?"

Even he thought he was pathetic for asking about that modest privilege.

⇔

A few minutes later

And so Nader stepped into the casino by himself.

He'd been to underground casinos in Chicago lots of times. The problem was that they might do things differently in New York. Besides, since the finer rules were different in each gambling den, he couldn't reliably base his conduct on past experience.

Thinking he should get a feel for the place first, Nader observed the surrounding gamblers. There were men and women of all ages, but of course, he didn't see any kids. The youngest person there seemed to be the guy in a green suit he'd glimpsed through the office window.

He wondered what a kid in his teens was doing down here, but since he'd been in the office, he was probably related to somebody on the staff.

If I manage to get that kid on my side, maybe I can break into this Martillo Family outfit.

The corners of Nader's mouth rose in a smirk even as the rest of his face went pale.

No, no, no! What am I saying? Am I an idiot?! That stuff is what landed me in this mess!

Scolding himself, Nader smacked his own face.

This was just for today.

By burning through this money, he'd turn over a new leaf and get out of the underworld.

If he vanished into the crowds of this great metropolis, even Huey's people wouldn't be able to find him.

Starting tomorrow, he was definitely going to look for honest work. They'd been talking about an assistant at a clinic back there… That wouldn't be bad.

Squeezing the wad of bills in his pocket, Nader imagined various tomorrows.

Still, he'd waded a significant way into underworld society, and he knew quite well that most people who resolved to go straight "tomorrow" ended up saying the same thing the next day. And the day after that, and the one after that… He knew tomorrow never came.

After all, if he'd been the type of person who could face tomorrow in a decent way, he wouldn't have been taking back roads like these in the first place.

⇔

In the office

"What's the matter, Firo?"

The young general manager had started shooting glances into the casino in the middle of their conversation, and Luck got curious.

"Sorry. New face, and he's acting weird. He was smacking himself. What's he doing?"

"Maybe it's his first time in a casino and he's trying to get himself fired up?"

"Oh, that could be… That's a bad sign, huh. I really am getting jumpy." Sighing, Firo turned back to Luck and began to explain. "You fellas got one, too, didn't you? One of those *invitations*."

"Yes, I'm afraid they weren't kind enough to overlook us. At any rate, we have a bit of history with them. If even unconnected organizations like the Martillos are being 'invited,' I suppose it was inevitable."

A few days earlier, just after Firo had finally managed to get back on the job, Molsa Martillo had abruptly summoned him and broached a certain subject.

"I expect you're aware that the Runorata Family is building a huge gambling den just next door to Manhattan."

Firo did know about that.

Rumors about it had been spreading before he went to jail.

A multipurpose building was going up on the coast of New York, near the island of Manhattan. It would house a hotel and shops, offices and restaurants—but people said the shadow of the Runorata Family was behind it.

All the land in that area was owned by Manfred Beriam, who had a notorious hatred of gangs, and even major mafia outfits had trouble establishing territories over there. However, in order to raise election funds, he'd put a portion of that land on the market. After traveling through several affluent parties, the rights had ended up in the hands of a corporation that was under the patronage of the Runoratas, and then the construction of that building had been announced.

Work on the building had proceeded rapidly, and while its height wouldn't set any records, its striking modern exterior made it clearly visible even from Manhattan Island.

In contrast to Nebula's Mist Wall, the structure was slender, with a design that tapered gradually. As a result, some wits had nicknamed it "Ra's Lance."

The building's unveiling ceremony had already been held. If his memory served him right, all that was left was the construction of part of the underground restaurant, which had been postponed. Under the restaurant, there were spare guest rooms for the hotel. It was said that the restaurant would mainly use them as private rooms for VIPs, but Firo had heard a rumor that those many VIP rooms would all be converted into gambling dens.

When Firo had recalled that much, Molsa had continued. "Those rumors even made it to you, and yet I haven't heard a word about the police making a move. Either they've gotten rid of just enough proof, or they've been handing out bribes here and there. This morning, a Runorata Family messenger came by. At first, I thought somebody was playing a trick on us, but it was no joke. Ronny recognized him, so it's a sure thing."

A messenger from the Runorata Family— What business could they have with a little outfit like ours? Firo had thought.

They couldn't have come to demand their territory, could they? Remembering how the Runoratas rumbled with the Gandors a few years earlier, Firo had been anxious. Molsa's following words had shaken him further.

"They said we're invited. And it isn't just us. They said they were going around to all the neighboring outfits. They're going to watch what the police do and set the date accordingly, but the casino's slated to open around the middle of February. All those underground rooms are going to be gambling dens. They've invited a crowd of big shots to the grand opening. On the day, they're going to let each outfit use one of those rooms, so they want us to get in there and profit…or so they say. What a screwball idea.

"I could have turned them down on my own say-so, but you're the one who's in charge of our gambling den now. So, Firo, you decide whether we're taking them up on their offer or not."

After spending a night mulling it over, Firo had told Molsa they'd accept. If he'd said he didn't want an opportunity to rebuild his reputation, he might have been lying.

However, Firo had taken this job because he thought it would ultimately benefit his family. Turning the offer down would have been an insult to the Runoratas.

Molsa hadn't appeared to care if this turned into a war, but Firo hadn't been able to stomach the idea of people thinking the Martillo Family had turned tail and run.

Of course, there was a definite possibility that it was a trap. He couldn't rule out the idea that the moment the executives showed up to run those underground gambling dens, they'd be met by Runorata hatchet men with machine guns.

The worst-case scenario was that the police would bust in while they were running the gambling dens, go through, and arrest every family member there. That would be more problematic than a machine-gun massacre. Even if Firo hadn't been immortal, he probably would have felt the same way.

After all, if they were formally arrested by the police, the cops could use that as a foothold to strike at every family involved. If the Runorata Family sacrificed the people they sent in for this scheme, then said they knew nothing and stuck to their story, they'd minimize the damage to themselves.

"If that happens, please tell them you cut me out of the family back when I went to jail. I swear I won't talk."

That was what Firo had told Molsa, when he went to let him know he'd decided to take the offer. Molsa had replied, "I wasn't planning on saying anything, either.

"If we find ourselves in that situation, I'll just slash the Runoratas' throats without a word."

⇔

"The damn Runorata Family, huh? They're huge, so they just do whatever they want," Firo groused to his old friend.

Luck listened with a wry smile. "Well, that is why they build up their strength in the first place," he said quietly.

"Buncha showoffs." Firo sighed. Then his expression turned

serious again. "Besides, it sounded like they wanted to make us their pigeons instead of just their bookies."

The Runorata messenger had said, *You're free to stake territory and concessions between syndicates. Naturally, if you'd like to gamble against us, any offer you make will be considered.*

"Doesn't that mean they just want to show off how much power they've got?" Firo asked. "If I had the time to let them yank me around like that, I'd just do the old-fashioned thing and lose on the sly to any fat cats who came to gamble."

"You'd lose?"

"If I let 'em win, they might bring all that money here, right?" Firo shrugged.

"...I hope it does go that well," Luck said. His face was expressionless. "I can't imagine there won't be strings."

"Sure. If they get the chance, they'll probably try to knock us down a few pegs in the eyes of everyone else around here."

"Naturally. Well, the venue itself is a gray zone, so you'll probably need to put some countermeasures in place."

"Yeah, Ronny told me, too. 'There's no knowing what might happen,' he said, 'so be careful.' That ain't gray. It's pitch-black."

Everyone in the family had absolute trust in Ronny's ability to gather information. He had a complete grasp of the executives of not only the surrounding gangs, but of mafia groups based on the West Coast. On top of that, his information had always been right.

It wasn't wise for an organization to rely on one person so completely. Even so, while they were drinking, Molsa had carelessly confided to Firo, *If Ronny sells us out, there won't be a thing we can do. It'll probably just mean I wasn't worthy of respect.* Even Firo thought that if Ronny turned traitor, they'd just have to give up.

Plus, nobody in the family had any idea why a guy with Ronny's skills was satisfied being an executive in a little outfit like theirs. They all thought it was bizarre. However, if they asked Ronny, all he'd say was *You overestimate me*, so Firo had decided Molsa was simply that charismatic.

Firo respected Molsa as a person, Maiza as a sort of older brother, and Ronny as someone about whom he could genuinely say, *He's a hell of a guy.* If Ronny was telling him to be careful, he didn't have the ghost of a reason to get careless.

That said, he didn't intend to back out.

"Still, I finally get out of stir and now this. Even if it is a coincidence, the timing's lousy."

He didn't regret it, but he did have a bone to pick with fate.

Looking away, Luck thought for a little while. Then he murmured to himself.

"…I'll be praying that it truly is just a coincidence."

⇔

Nader had been observing people while pretending to take a breather in a corner of the casino.

He'd considered getting in on a card game, but his right hand was a prosthetic. It was a specially designed, Nebula-made prosthetic, and since he'd trained with it, he could do things like set his hand on a steering wheel or hold a wine glass with it in a way that looked natural, but he couldn't manage the fine motions it would take to handle cards.

He wanted to avoid standing out by playing one-handed for a while longer. Once eyes were on him, he wouldn't have the technique or the courage to calmly observe his observers in return. For now, Nader had decided he'd watch the room for ten more minutes, then take a seat at a roulette table or something, when—

"How are you making out?"

The man who'd spoken was standing right next to him. There was no telling when he'd gotten there, and all Nader's hair stood on end.

"?!"

Thinking the guy might be a hitman who'd marked him, he reflexively covered his throat and heart with his arms.

"That's an interesting startle reflex."

"N-no, uh, sorry." He apologized automatically. However, since it was still possible that the man was after him, he checked him out cautiously.

At a glance, the other guy seemed to be a few years younger than he was, maybe still in his teens. He was probably about the same age as the boy he'd seen through the office window earlier.

"No, no. I'm sorry I startled you. As an apology, would you care for a chip?" The boy handed him one of the cheapest slot tokens.

"Nah, don't worry about it."

"It's fine. Go on. Think of it as a lucky chip and give it a spin." The boy glanced at the slot machine right beside them.

"...I'll take you up on that, then. Thanks."

This boy might have ties to the gambling den, too. If so, it probably wouldn't be a good idea to keep turning him down. Deciding to casually test his luck, Nader dropped the token into that slot machine.

The reels spun.

The afterimages of the assorted pictures merged together, making it look as though three rainbow-colored rivers were flowing side by side.

Nader didn't have any particular knowledge about slots, so he watched those rainbows until the spinning stopped, his mind elsewhere.

With a pleasant noise, the first drum halted.

From the sound, one would have thought the slot machine had become a musical instrument. The silvery bell that rang out whenever a drum stopped made Nader's heart shiver.

[7]

Wow. So that's what slots are like these days?

[7]

When I was making money chiseling casinos, they were nothing like—

[7]

—this, but...bu...bu...bu...?

At that point, for a moment, Nader's mind went completely blank.

Three sevens. There were three [7] pictures, all in a row.

Before Nader could remember what getting a total of twenty-one meant—

Evolving from a singular instrument into an orchestra, the Nebula-made slot machine sent the original music that announced a jackpot echoing through the casino.

⟺

"Wh-what's that noise?"

The music certainly wasn't dark or foreboding, but it had begun blaring up to them from below just as their group started down the stairs, and Jacuzzi involuntarily shrank back.

Ronny, who was in the lead, answered him with no emotion on his face. "Hmm… It sounds as though someone's hit a jackpot on the slots."

"A jackpot?! That's incredible!" Jacuzzi's eyes shone with envy.

Ronny continued down the stairs, smiling wryly.

"It isn't a sound proprietors really want to hear, but… Well, never mind."

⟺

"Goddammit, that guy!"

When Firo heard the noise, then realized the man in front of the slot machine was that new customer, he sprang to his feet.

"Calm down, Firo. It could be coincidence. Besides, you were just telling me that it wasn't a problem if someone hit a jackpot on that model," Luck said.

"Yeah, but come on. He's fishy… Plus, that was the triple seven music, the top jackpot. Even if you put all the slots together, you get one of those every ten days, but someone just got one yesterday!"

"In terms of probability, you can't say you'd never get one two days in a row. If you're suspicious of him but it turns out to be simple coincidence, it'll be the Martillo Family name that will suffer, not yours."

"…Yeah, I know. I know that. I'm not gonna walk up and deck him."

Firo, who'd calmed down a bit at Luck's words, started toward the door that led into the hall and took a few deep breaths.

"I'll just go congratulate him and get a feel for what's going on."

⟺

"H-hey..."

This reel machine seemed to be a bit special.

As flashy music played on multiple bells, tokens poured out of the machine's payout window. These weren't like the bottom-rung token Nader had put in. They were the most expensive type this underground casino used.

In this era, slot machines weren't controlled electronically, like the ones that would be made in the latter half of the twentieth century. Even the house couldn't adjust the probability. Compared to the models that would emerge later, the odds of lining up the top roll were relatively high, so as payouts went, it wasn't that abnormal.

Even so, it had given him enough chips that if he lived frugally, he'd easily be able to eat for a year without working. In this recession, it really was a ridiculous sum.

"Well, congratulations!" As Nader stood stunned, the boy who'd handed him the token complimented him. Then he started clapping. Everyone in the casino except those who were in the middle of their games turned to see what the fuss was about. The building erupted into thunderous applause.

In the midst of a storm of adulation, the likes of which he'd never experienced before in his life, Nader was drenched in cold sweat.

No.

He was just an average guy of no importance. He knew that as a fundamental truth.

There's no way I have this kind of luck, he told himself.

No matter what his actual luck might be, he wasn't the type who hit the jackpot.

It had to be this kid. This must be some sort of stunt...!

In other words, he had been dragged into something.

And the smiling boy in front of him had made him draw a *stupendous* booby prize.

As if to confirm his hunch, another boy appeared in front of Nader's dazed eyes. "Congratulations, sir!"

Huh? He's...the kid who was looking out of the office window.

"Sir"...? So what, does he work here or something?

No, wait, why would a rank-and-file employee be talking to me like this?

The boy in the pale-green suit greeted Nader respectfully. "I'm Firo Prochainezo, the manager here. I'm glad someone as fortunate as you found your way to our establishment. I can only hope some of that excellent luck will rub off on us."

Anyone who knew the regular Firo would have busted a gut. *Who'd he crib those highfalutin lines from?!* they'd laugh. Nader was meeting him for the first time, though, and he couldn't believe what he was hearing.

Huh?

H-he's the manager? How old is this guy?!

Nader was close to drowning in the surge of questions through his mind, but he managed to hang in there and say what needed to be said. "Oh, no, you've got it wrong..."

"Wrong? What do you mean?"

"This was his..." As Nader spoke, he pointed at the boy who'd handed him the token—or at least he tried to. By the time he turned around, the kid was gone; he'd disappeared into the applauding crowd.

He's...! I knew it!

I was right. That kid—he set me up!

An ordinary person might have thought of the boy as an angel who'd brought them good luck, but to Nader, he was a jinx who'd shone the worst kind of spotlight in him. He suspected he was about to be plunged into the sort of trouble that a jackpot couldn't begin to make up for.

"Is something the matter?"

"Oh, no... It's nothing." The color had drained from Nader's face.

As Firo spoke to him, that breezy smile was still pasted on his face. "By the way, sir... May I ask who referred you to this casino?"

Although the place wasn't completely invitation-only since it was an illegal casino, they didn't get any customers who just "happened to wander in." After all, there was no signage, and at a glance, the entrance looked like the back door of a general store.

Getting anxious, Nader groped around for an answer. Then he realized he'd heard the name "Firo" before.

Th-that's right. Of course. Ladd said his friend ran this casino. This kid is the friend, huh?!

"Fr-from Ladd! Ladd Russo! He said he was a pal of yours!"

With a huge smile, as if he'd managed to catch himself on the brink of disaster, Nader gave him the name, but—

Conversely, Firo's smile turned icy and tense.

Uh?!

That's not how people react to a friend's name!

He felt like screaming *This isn't what you told me!* at Ladd, but despite the greasy sweat building on his skin, he managed to suppress the feeling and smile.

"Sir...," Firo said. "You mean *they let him out*?"

⟺

By the casino entrance

"What are you going to do, Ennis? Aren't you going in?"

"But...I might end up getting in Firo's way when he's working..."

In the end, Ennis had stopped in the road in front of the casino, unsure whether to intrude. As she eyed the casino's entrance uneasily, Annie spurred her on. "It's fine, Ennis! We'll walk in as customers. Just hold your head high and go right in."

"But something dangerous might happen. Czes and Annie, you should probably go home..."

At that, Annie pouted irritably, then pinched Ennis's cheeks.

"Wha' ah oo 'ooin'?"

"I swear! It would be just as dangerous for you, Ennis!"

After thoroughly squeezing, pinching, and messing with Ennis's cheeks, Annie let go. "You and I are both delicate, fragile girls!" she said emphatically. "That means the playing field is level!"

"Playing field? What playing field?"

"......"

In that moment, a silent wind blustered between them.

Ennis cocked her head, perplexed, while Annie blushed a little. Neither said a word.

When a man ran between them into the casino, Annie finally broke the awkward silence. "...Aw, geez! Why are you and Firo both so apathetic?!"

"I'm sorry. I don't know what this is about, but it sounds as if I've caused you trouble... Firo isn't apathetic, though. He's quite earnest and attentive to many things."

"......"

Ennis and Annie continued their noncommittal conversation. They seemed likely to just stay the whole night there outside without making any progress.

"Um, listen, you two?" Czes cut in, destroying the mood. "I don't think now is the time for this."

What he said next was extremely ominous.

"The man who just went into the casino was carrying a big gun."

⇔

Inside the casino

Firo was in front of the slot machines, talking with a customer.

From the foot of the stairs, Ronny watched them wordlessly. Jacuzzi and Christopher were going along with the rest of the crowd and clapping, but Firo didn't seem to have noticed them. The children's faces were unimpressed, but Ricardo was applauding politely.

"A jackpot! Wow. Lucky..." Jacuzzi was genuinely jealous.

"He doesn't look too happy, though," Rail said. "By the way, is Firo the one who looks like a kid?"

Ronny put a finger to his lips, warning them in a low voice. "He has a complex about that baby face. If you don't want to get hurt, I wouldn't mention it in front of him... I doubt he's so hot-tempered that he'd truly lose his temper at a child, but you'll definitely sour his mood."

"...How about that. I'll be careful." Rail replied indifferently, but she still stopped smiling and looked away. Ronny had that effect.

"Huh...? Wait, is he older than I am?" Jacuzzi asked. He was lucky that Firo wasn't nearby to overhear him and knock him out.

However, Jacuzzi never got an answer from Ronny.

After all, that was when the employee who'd been keeping an eye on the ground-level entrance came tumbling down the stairs with a crash.

⇔

"So what did Ladd say when he told you about this place?" Firo asked, his eyes twitching.

Nader was racking his brains for a response when a loud noise abruptly came from the direction of the entrance, and a boy with a tattooed face screamed.

"What's going on?" Firo whirled around toward the source of the noise, and his eyes landed on the foot of the stairs. One thing immediately caught his attention: a red-eyed monster who was flashing a fanged, vicious smile and waving at him.

.........*?!*

"Ghk...! Christopher?!" he blurted out.

What's he doing here?!

He was too surprised to do anything initially, but a moment later, he caught sight of the man on the floor behind the monster. His first thought was that Christopher had caused this, but it looked like the guy had tumbled down the stairs just a second ago.

Next, he saw a man with a nearly demonic expression descending the stairs, gripping a tommy gun.

Firo recognized the guy—he'd just busted him for cheating, slugged him, and booted him out. The guy was supposed to have been taken to the Martillos' office, but he must have managed to make a break for it.

"Dam mavya bassars!"

The cheater—who had a crushed throat, courtesy of Firo—brandished the tommy gun he'd picked up somewhere, firing wildly at the ceiling. Shots rang out, and an uproar punctuated with screams ballooned inside the casino.

Son of a bitch...! He's gone off the rails!

From the fact that he hadn't had any trouble getting his hands on a tommy gun, he might belong to a mafia outfit somewhere. Still, no syndicate anywhere would protect a guy who'd gotten caught cheating, been punished for it, and then pulled a stunt like this in retaliation.

Does this fella have a death wish? Did getting his ass handed to him frustrate him that much?

Or...did he think that because it's the Martillo Family, he could do whatever he wants here and still make a clean getaway?

Either way, I'm gonna make him wish he'd never been born.

"Waaaugh-agh-agh-agh-agh?!"

The fact that a man had appeared right behind him and fired a tommy gun at random sent Jacuzzi into a total panic. Rail and Ricardo only covered their ears; they didn't seem particularly rattled. As Christopher waited to see how Firo would handle the gunman, his eyes shone. Ronny didn't seem at all disturbed. He chose not to immediately neutralize the thug, hoping to avoid using his powers in front of a crowd.

The man who'd fallen down the stairs didn't seem to have been shot. The other man had probably threatened him with the gun, then kicked him down. Once he was certain the Martillo man was only unconscious, Ronny breathed a sigh of relief.

All right. What should I do? he thought. *For the moment, maybe I'll simply jump on the man and subdue him in the normal way.*

If he had to, he could make the gun vanish from the man's hands like a mirage. In front of this particular crowd, though, insisting it had been a magic trick probably wouldn't go as smoothly as it had with Jacuzzi's gang.

On that thought, he was planning to act like Firo's "knife-fighting teacher" for once and reached into his jacket for his blade—but then something he witnessed brought him to a halt.

How about that. I won't be needed this time, hmm?

Well, never mind.

He sighed, smiling faintly.

A woman in a black men's suit was leaping down from the top of the stairs.

"Ah!" "Ahn?" "Aaaah!" "Ah—" "...Ah."

With the exception of the shooter, nearly everyone—including Firo, Nader, Jacuzzi, Rail, and Ricardo—reacted at once.

The gunman hesitated a moment, realizing that all the eyes around him were focused on something over his head.

By the time he noticed, it was too late.

Before he even had time to look up, a sharp impact ran through him.

The woman in the black suit had brought her right leg down on the man's collarbone. Then she grabbed the gun, which had been pointed at the ceiling moments prior, and she wrenched it upward along with his arm.

The man's collarbone broke with a nasty crunch, and almost immediately afterward, there was a disturbing pop as his right shoulder was dislocated.

The thug opened his mouth to scream in pain just in time for the butt of his gun to be slammed into it.

All his teeth broke, and he blacked out before he even saw the face of the individual who'd stopped him.

The attacker had been subdued far too easily and much too efficiently.

The casino's guests were stunned for a moment—but then they showered the woman with applause befitting a hero, far more than the cheers for Nader's jackpot.

Meanwhile, Ennis looked around, spotted Firo, and gave a small sigh of relief. On the other hand, Firo wondered what Ennis was doing there, although he was relieved that she was safe and the situation resolved.

"...Huh? It's over? It's done already? And here I thought we were going to get a show!"

The only dissatisfied comment came from Christopher. Resolving to get the full story out of him later, Firo took a closer look at the area around the stairs. Spotting Ronny, Firo froze up guiltily.

Aaaaaagh! Dammit!

Ronny just saw me screw up!

Firo hadn't done anything wrong, but as the manager of this casino, the very fact that something like this had happened was a disgrace... Or that was how Firo saw it anyway.

He still figured getting the situation under control was more important than his shame, though, so he raised his voice and addressed the crowd. "I'm very sorry for the disturbance, folks! Those gunshots may have attracted the cops. We'll get your chips cashed right away, so for now, go ahead and call it a day."

The cops.

At the mention of law enforcement, the guests turned pale.

"My sincere apologies to those of you who were on a roll and those who were trying to dig themselves out of a hole. I swear we'll make it up to you another day, so please do us a favor and head home for now."

Even as Firo finished his sentence, the customers scrambled over one another to mob the cashier, while gamblers who'd lost and become simple onlookers rushed for the exit. They probably weren't satisfied, but they had no time to gripe to Firo or the others. Rather than run the risk of being dragged into police business, many gamblers who still had a few chips left headed for the exit anyway.

As he directed traffic, Firo grumbled to himself, *...This just cost us half our customers.*

Because underground casinos were illegal, trust from gamblers was particularly vital. It was one thing if the gambling den belonged to the organization that ran the town, but here in Manhattan, multiple outfits had opened their own casinos. If something unpleasant happened at one, guests could easily take their business to another outfit's establishment.

We'll have to win their trust back somehow. Firo ground his teeth.

Behind him, he heard Ennis speaking to him. "Are you all right, Firo?"

He was planning to play it cool and say something like, *I'm in the middle of evacuating customers. It's an important job. We'll talk later*—but the moment he saw Ennis's face, those words evaporated.

"Y-yeah. I'm fine. Never mind that; you're not hurt, are you, Ennis?" Even as he said it, he realized it was a pointless question to ask an immortal.

"I'm fine. When I heard the shots, I thought someone had been hurt."

"Well, he only shot up the ceiling. Unlike Alveare, the first story of this place has a sturdy floor, so I doubt any bullets even punched through."

Firo tried to keep directing customers during their conversation, but another person intruded.

"Hiya, Firo. Tough luck, huh. Or does that sort of thing happen all the time?"

A red-eyed phantom poked his head out from behind Ennis.

"Christopher… What are you doing here?" Thoroughly disgruntled, Firo decided to deal with him absently and keep working.

Christopher responded to this reception with an exaggerated shrug. "Aww, so mean. Is that any way to treat a close friend you haven't seen in ages?"

"I don't see this close friend anywhere."

"C'mon, don't be rude. We're going to be working together again, you know."

"Hunh?" At that unexpected news, Firo stopped waving customers through and turned to face Christopher. "What are you talking about? Don't tell me— Are you planning to do something crazy again, like you did at Mist Wall?"

"Hey, that's entirely up to you."

Christopher's evasiveness made Firo tense again, but that was when someone else appeared beside him and broke into their conversation.

"It's a pleasure to meet you, Mr. Firo Prochainezo."

"…?"

The speaker was a child who seemed to be a few years older than Czes. What was a kid doing here?

As Firo wondered about that, the child coolly went on. "My name is Ricardo Russo. On instructions from Molsa Martillo, Christopher and I will be working under you from now on. We're both looking forward to it."

"Huh?"

Ricardo...Russo?

On Molsa's instructions? Working under me?

Christopher, too?

Firo had no idea what was going on, but the name "Russo" reminded him of what the customer who'd hit the triple seven a few minutes earlier had said. "Oh, right, where'd he go...? I—I'll hear you out later, so sit tight a minute."

Hastily excusing himself to Ricardo, Firo scanned the room. The jackpot winner was just about to cash the tokens the slot machine had paid out.

Firo started over to him, walking fast.

As she watched him go, Ricardo murmured, "He'll hear us out later, huh?"

With her eyes focused on some place that wasn't here, Ricardo went on talking to herself.

"I hope we'll have time in the chaos later."

⇔

Outside the casino By the entrance

"I wonder if Ennis is okay..."

"The gunshots stopped. That probably means she's all right."

Customers were hastily running up the casino stairs to the entrance, then scattering in all directions.

"But we heard those shots loud and clear, so...the police are bound to be here soon."

"I wouldn't be so sure. I think they're busy right now."

"?"

As Czes and Annie were talking, they heard a jaunty voice behind them. "Hey, kid. Hey, little lady. Those were some flashy firecrackers I heard just now. Was that from in there?"

"Huh?" Czes tensed as he turned to see who was talking to them.

Several men and a woman were standing back there...and he'd recognized one of the men.

When the man saw Czes's face, he seemed to realize something, too. He smiled at him, but his eyebrows came together. "Hmm...? Have we met somewhere before, kid? You look familiar."

The man thought hard for a few more seconds, but then, before he'd remembered completely, he headed for the casino entrance. "Ah, whatever. Right now, I need to put in an appearance at that party." Just then, out of the corner of his eye, he registered the fact that the girl had fixed him with a ferocious glare. Stopping for a moment, he seemed mystified. "Hmm? What is it, little lady? I haven't met you before, have I?"

That girl, Annie, didn't respond. She only radiated hostility, glaring at the man as if he'd killed her parents.

"Did I bump off your fella somewhere, dollface? If so, sorry 'bout that. Not that I regret it or anything," he said, amused by her nasty expression. He set off again, his retinue trailing behind him.

"I can tell you're holding some sort of grudge there. Sorry, sweetheart, but if you're planning to slaughter me, follow me down to the party."

⇔

Inside the casino

"...So you thought we'd just let you head on home?"

Nader had finished cashing in his chips, but Firo blocked his way, wearing a hearty smile. Of course, that smile didn't reach his eyes. Most of the twenty or so gamblers who'd been there had already booked it outside, and the casino staff was tying the grifter up.

Hugging an armful of bundled bills, Nader shook his head and pleaded with him. "H-hey... Hold on a minute. Check into it and you'll see. I didn't cheat or nothin'."

"Well, let's set that aside for now. What I'm curious about is the guy who told you about this place. Ladd."

Watching their conversation from a short distance away, Christopher shook his head. He seemed bored. "This really isn't what I was hoping for. You said it was Firo's casino, so I thought they'd be playing Russian roulette with Gatling guns or something."

"...Firo doesn't look like that much of a dimwit to me."

"Once you're the boss, Ricardo, let's build an underground casino that shows more respect for Nature. It'll have incredibly big slot machines that use waterfalls, and roulette games that use tornadoes."

"I don't intend to be that much of a dimwit, either," Ricardo responded sullenly. She paused for just a moment, then added, "By the way, Christopher..."

"Hmm? What?"

"I recommend you turn around *soon*."

"?"

As she made that bizarre remark, Ricardo was still looking ahead. Christopher turned to look back—

—and saw a lethal silver disc flying straight at him.

He'd seen this same thing at the end of last year, in a restaurant in Chicago.

Christopher's kinetic vision managed to register that the object wasn't actually a silver plate but an enormous wrench. It was spinning so fast that it left a disc-shaped afterimage.

At the same time, he saw a young man partway down the stairs, wearing blue coveralls and a crazed smile.

"...Ha!"

Confronted with a sudden, incoming mass of death, Christopher broke into a fiendish smile of his own and vigorously kicked the enormous wrench upward.

With a dull clang, the wrench bounced into the air, its rotation broken.

"What's that?"

"Hunh...?"

Firo and Nader saw the altercation in their periphery. When they turned to see what was happening, they saw something almost incomprehensible: Christopher and a man in blue on the stairs were simultaneously smiling and glaring at each other, while a wrench as big as a human arm fell between them.

The next moment, the huge tool landed on the back of the cheater, who'd been tied up and left on the ground nearby.

"Gebwaugh?!"

It hit the man's spine, and he let out an unconscious shriek before succumbing to a quiet blackout again.

Tumbling off the man's back, the wrench hit the floor with a loud clatter, and the handful of remaining gamblers curiously glanced their way.

"Fun... Let me tell you a fun story," announced the man in the blue coveralls.

Graham completely disregarded the uncomfortable reactions from those around him and jumped onto the stair rail, nimbly balancing on top of it. His voice echoed through the whole place.

"Today, I stepped into this casino to gamble. I've heard casinos are life in a microcosm, and gambling dens are a competition with your own life in the balance... And looky here: I hit the jackpot! I knew I'd face my fated rival again. I'm talking about the vaguely irritating red-eyed bastard. To think we'd run into each other here!"

After that lengthy speech, Graham took normal-sized wrenches from his waist and began juggling them. They smacked into his hand on each catch.

"If reunions are jackpots, well, I just reunited with my brother Ladd, too, so I've won twice in a row! I feel like I drew the lucky seven card... If I reunite with one more card... Yeah, on the day I meet my big sister. Haven't heard from her in forever. Then, I'll have three lucky sevens, get a jackpot on the slots, win at blackjack with twenty-one, and victory will be mine! Could any story be more fun?"

Graham had delivered that incomprehensible monologue in time to his own rhythm. When he reached its finale, he pulled the wrenches out of circulation with light smacks, catching them in both hands.

"In other words, I'm thinking of pulling all your teeth and using them as chips. That okay with you?"

He sprang forward from the stairs, lunging at Christopher.

It was an astounding jump, and he covered a distance of several yards easily. Spinning without killing his momentum, Graham tried to slam his wrenches into Christopher.

However, Christopher dodged them at the last second, leaping to the side. "Wow. That opinion's so selfish it's genuinely moving! What'll I do?"

His question made him sound indecisive, but in no time at all, he launched himself off the floor, rotating at an angle, and unleashed a spinning kick.

Graham evaded by flinging himself back into an exaggerated bridge pose and went on the attack, holding that position as he lobbed a wrench at the airborne Christopher.

Christopher snatched it out of the air easily and touched down as cleanly as a gymnast. "Nah, it's not okay with me. Quit gambling and go straight. Then your sister might come back, you know."

"What…? My sis?! Okay, got it! I'm on the straight and narrow! No more gambling for me!"

Christopher had been taunting him, but Graham responded in dead earnest. Springing back up from his bridge, he transferred his momentum into a pointless somersault over to his enormous wrench. He brandished it and his little wrench as if they were two swords, clanked them together, then rushed at Christopher again.

"By the way, my sister was also my first crush. When I see her again, should I call her Sissy or Sis or Sister or My Honey or Damn Hag? Whaddaya think? This is a pretty thrilling gamble. If I happen to tick her off, she might dismantle my spine using nothing but her upper body strength." Graham kept on flapping his mouth with each swing of a wrench.

Dodging by the skin of his teeth or parrying with the little wrench he held in his right hand, Christopher responded cheerfully. "You really are dumb, huh! That's fine! Even if they mobilized all their reason and intelligence, humans can't get away from gambling. It's in your nature. In other words, it's the instinct of the species... Instinct of the species—somehow, that's sounds so natural, doesn't it?! Meaning that for humans, this casino is no different from forests or grasslands or the vast ocean!"

As always, Christopher had his own unique theory.

Both Christopher and Graham were about as broken as the other, but their gears would never mesh. They collided with a crunching noise that would frighten anyone with a sound mind. Even gamblers who hadn't yet cashed in their chips began to rush outside.

With the screams and clamor of the scrambling customers as its soundtrack, the fight kept heating up.

On the sidelines of that fight, a variety of human reactions played out. Ronny listened to their exchange with deep interest. Rail said, "I've got to help Chris," and took a bomb out of her jacket. The crying Jacuzzi tried to stop her, while Ennis struggled to process the situation.

At first, Firo had been stunned and bewildered, too, but when he saw his screaming customers heading for the exit, he came to himself with a jolt. He hadn't managed to get a handle on the situation at all, but if this kept up, his casino's reputation would take another dive. Firo bellowed at the combatants and their ferocious sword fight with wrenches. "Whoa, whoa, whoa, hold up a minute, fellas! No, y'know what? Freeze, both of you!"

Maybe they'd heard him, maybe they hadn't, but Christopher and the man in blue showed no sign of calling off their fight. Thinking he'd just have to stop them by force, Firo reached into his jacket for his knife, but just then—

From beside him, Ricardo softly put a hand on his arm, holding him back. "It's okay. Let them be. They'll get tired and stop before long."

Calmly, Firo argued with the child. "N-no, if I wait until that happens, my casino's going to get smashed to..."

However, Ricardo glanced at the top of the stairs without much of a reaction. "Isn't he the person you really need to talk to?"

"Huh?"

Following Ricardo's gaze, Firo looked at the stairs—then froze.

Potential trouble even greater than the two brawlers was standing there, smiling a gleeful smile.

"Hey there, Peter Pan. It's been, what, two months or so?"

"...Ladd. What, you got out already?"

It was a man he'd met in Alcatraz.

It was the first time he'd seen Ladd in clothes other than his prison uniform. The air of danger that hung around him might have been even greater now than it had been in the big house.

"Yeah, they just turned me loose today. So, this is your Neverland, huh? Nice, real nice. Li'l punks who never grow up gambling forever—that's a pretty entertaining thought! Ain't it, Lua?"

"It sounds like a wonderful world." The woman behind Ladd spoke quietly and smiled.

Oh... Um. Right, she's Ladd's fiancée. She's more of a looker than I expected.

At the sight of this woman, Lua—whose name he'd heard ad nauseam in prison—Firo felt momentarily relieved. She'd almost been taken hostage by Sham and Hilton, but apparently these two had managed to find each other again.

Jolting back to his senses, he remembered this was no time to be feeling anything like relief. "Hey, is that fella in blue with you? Make him knock it off already!"

"Ha-ha-ha! No can do. Once he gets like that, he won't stop unless you splash liquor on him or something. Fights to the death are one thing, but in regular ol' fights, he's stronger'n me," Ladd said bluntly, leaving Firo without a paddle.

"Enough. I'll stop him myself, then."

"Whew! You're planning to stick your head into that wrenchnado? Damn. Rough work, bein' a manager."

Thoroughly irritated with Ladd, who'd decided to rubberneck and enjoy the show, Firo gave a little sigh before he sized up the situation. True, both men were moving in ways no ordinary person could. Firo knew about five people who had the skills to stop people of that caliber. That said, the fact that there were five such people in his circle meant that Firo knew a lot of abnormal individuals.

One of those people, Ronny, was simply watching the fight as if it fascinated him. Maybe, since Firo was the one in charge here and the customers had escaped to safety, he simply wasn't planning to interfere.

Either way, Firo was young and proud, and that pride wouldn't have let him run crying to Ronny while Ennis was there.

Warily, Firo went closer to the fight. Behind him, Nader called to Ladd: "Didn't you go to a hospital or some such to see your old pal?"

"They were closed today."

The answer was extremely simple and clear, and it was enough to convince him.

Behind Graham was a very enervated Shaft. That concerned Nader, but not so much that he'd go out of his way to ask him what had happened.

Just then, Ladd noticed the bundles of bills in Nader's arms. "...Hey, whoa, get out, are you kidding me?! Something wild went down here! That's about ten times the money I handed you! What the hell?! Man, that's really somethin'! Nader, pal, you're a riot! Did my uncle have the curse on you because you busted his casinos?"

When he heard that phrase, Firo twitched and glared at Nader. "...You're a casino breaker?"

"N-no! I've never cheated at a casino! Besides, the one who's really famous for breaking casinos in Chicago was a jane named Pamela, and you know it!"

As Nader shouted, Graham's wrench slammed into the floor, sending a violent noise echoing through the casino.

Without seeming to care, Ladd latched on to the name "Pamela."

"Hmm? Oh, right, yeah, yeah, that's the one. Pamela, it was Pamela. My uncle put a bounty on her, too, and she made tracks. I wonder what she's up to now?"

As they talked about things that wouldn't have made sense to anyone who didn't know much about Chicago, one person interrupted to answer Ladd's question. "I heard a lady named Pamela pulled off a museum heist somewhere and is on the run from the police as well."

"Hunh?"

Ladd gave the speaker a hard look, and then his face lit up.

"Huh? Hey, Ricardo! It's you, huh? Well, look at that! You've gotten big since I saw you last. So I hear you took over the Russo Family. That's gonna be one hell of a job."

"Did you want it? ...The family."

"Hell nah. I didn't get along with my uncle's cronies, that Krieck louse and his men. Nobody says I gotta take on a hassle like that, and plus, if I was the boss, I couldn't be a hitman." Ladd, who'd become a hired killer for the fun of it, wouldn't have taken the boss's chair if they'd paid him. "Still, from what they tell me, it's just you and that red-eyed nutjob, right? If you need a hit, call me up whenever. We're family, so I'll do the job for you cheap."

"...I don't plan to repeat Grandpa Placido's mistakes." Ricardo shook her head quietly. There was no hatred in her eyes, but they were firmly rejecting the offer. The Russo Family she was going to build wouldn't need people like Ladd. She'd told him so, plainly, right to his face.

However, Ladd didn't seem particularly ticked off. He laughed. "Ha! That's one wholesome mafia outfit. Well, I guess it's better than Uncle Placido anyway. All right, I'll start working freelance here in New York, then."

Ladd continued down the stairs, watching the scene that was unfolding below, when—he suddenly caught sight of a guy who was staring at him from a corner of the casino and trembling. It was a kid with an inked-up face. The moment Ladd saw that tattoo, he remembered exactly who he was.

"Well, well! Ain't that Jacuzzi Splot over there?"

* * *

"Eeeep!"

H-he remembers meeee!

The moment their eyes met, the man had called his name. Despair flooded Jacuzzi's expression, and sweat broke out on his back. He'd known they'd probably run into each other, but he'd never dreamed it would happen out of nowhere, here of all places.

"C'mon! I drop in to see my pal Firo and get a load of this! Did you fellas set up a surprise party here, just for me? Why is a bounty whooping it up at a casino with the boss of the Russo Family?"

Lightly descending the stairs, Ladd started toward Jacuzzi with slow, menacing steps.

Th-this Firo guy has a ton of dangerous friends... What's going on?!

Silently screaming a question that entirely ignored his own circumstances, Jacuzzi spoke up fearfully. "H-hello. It's been a long time."

"If I recall, on the train, you said, uh, lemme see... Something about absolutely making me pay. Ain't that right?"

"Yeeeek?!"

He even remembers that?!

"So how are you planning to do it? Want to put that plan into action right here?"

The words were taunting, and a shudder ran all through Jacuzzi.

Apologize.

That voice echoed up from the depths of his heart.

He'd made that challenge in the heat of the moment. If he asked Ladd to forget it, promised to grovel or do whatever he wanted, and begged for forgiveness, the man might not actually kill him.

That was what Jacuzzi's rational brain was telling him, but the memory of Jack near death rose in his mind, and he shoved that option back into the depths of his heart. Although there were tears in Jacuzzi's eyes, the next thing he said was: "I—I'll make you pay by, um... I—I'm still deciding! Please look forward to it!"

At that outrageous answer, not only Ladd, but also Firo and even Nader stared openmouthed at Jacuzzi.

However, in the next moment, Ladd chuckled. "You really are something, fella. Good thing I didn't kill you on that train, yeah?"

Jacuzzi had no idea how to react, and he fell silent.

Graham had overheard their conversation, and he yelled to Ladd. "Oh— Ladd! I've got something to tell you about that Jacuzzi guy later, so don't kill him! He's my pal! And hey, Jacuzzi, what're you doing here? Should I see this...as my third reunion card...? We just saw each other the other day, though..."

Pausing his attack for a moment after shouting to Ladd, Graham switched to talking to himself.

This created a prime opening for Christopher. He grabbed that chance—but he didn't use it to attack Graham.

With a grin, he raised the wrench he was holding and lobbed it at the back of *Ladd's* head.

"Aaaaah, look out!!"

Luckily for Ladd, his enemy Jacuzzi tipped him off about the impending crisis. Jacuzzi's already pale face went even paler, and as he screamed, Ladd *raised his left arm and turned around.*

The next moment, a peculiar crash rang out.

Ladd's iron prosthetic hand had solidly protected his head from the flying wrench, with the sleeve of his suit jacket sandwiched in the middle.

"Thanks. I owe you one," Ladd told Jacuzzi, cracking his neck.

Meanwhile, the wrench he'd deflected sailed through the air, heading toward Rail. Rail dodged, and Ennis stepped in front of her, then kicked the wrench to the ground.

When Rail said nothing, Ennis asked, "Are you all right?"

"...Nobody asked you to butt in," Rail retorted sullenly, apparently having a bone to pick with Ennis. However, she'd spoken normally, and Ennis smiled in relief.

"Oh, good. It looks like you're okay."

"......!"

"Wow. Rail doesn't know what to do when people treat her like that."

As Christopher watched Rail, who was wearing a complicated

expression, he gave a mischievous grin. He'd forgotten the stunt he'd just pulled.

Tilting his head to one side, Graham looked at Christopher. He, on the other hand, was not smiling.

"...Huh? Why did you just take a shot at my brother Ladd?"

"I wondered how you'd react if somebody you apparently respect got hurt."

"...That's it?"

"That's it. ☺"

Christopher smiled like a naughty little kid. Instantly, every inch of Graham began radiating murder.

That is, until he picked up on an even more overwhelming hostility from behind him. Graham shuddered.

"I see. That's a real simple answer. I like it," Ladd said. Smiling cheerfully, merrily, he asked Christopher a question: "Then it's okay if I jump in here, right?"

"Be my guest. ♪" "Ladd, this guy's mine..."

Christopher and Graham spoke at the exact same time, but Ladd wasn't listening to either of them.

Brrr...

Jacuzzi, Ennis, and Rail had seen Ladd's face, and a chill ran down their spines.

Though he was smiling, behind it was pure bloodlust.

It was a self-sustaining system of warped pleasure, in which the sheer opportunity to turn that urge to kill on somebody was way too much fun in his mind.

Firo had a feeling how this would turn out, and he tried to shut it down in advance. "H-hey..."

But with that as the signal, Ladd took off.

A single step.

The other two were five meters away.

Christopher's opportunity to brace himself was canceled out by just one step.

"Hey, red-eyed bastard."

Ladd closed in, staying low. He greeted him casually, and in almost the same moment, he unleashed a unique, upward right jab.

"?!"

It was a high-speed first strike, something Ladd's rather large frame hadn't seemed capable of.

Overwhelmed by the speed worthy of a pro boxer, Christopher reflexively pulled back.

As Ladd stretched his right arm to its limit, he took one more step forward. His right hand instantly shifted from a fist to a claw, latching on to Christopher's throat.

Christopher visualized his head being crushed by a monster punch.

Huh? Is this when I die? he asked himself.

The pressure on his neck was abnormal. Christopher raised a foot, preparing to strike back, but Ladd took another step in. Still holding Christopher by the throat, he jumped forward and swung Christopher's body as lightly as if it were a bucket.

After whipping Christopher around at a speed that could easily have dislocated an ordinary person's neck, Ladd slammed him into a roulette table.

The table broke right in two.

"Aaaaaaaaaaaah! Goddammit, what the hell are you doing?!" Firo screamed. He was thinking of how much it would cost to replace the table and the losses they'd incur while it was out of commission. However, he didn't seem particularly worried about Christopher; he knew this wouldn't be enough to kill him.

As a matter of fact, although Christopher was being pinned down by the throat between the pieces of the broken roulette table, he was still smiling.

Ladd smiled back. "Listen, fella, do you think you're not about to die or somethin'?"

"No, I'm not so sure about that. If I die, it'll mean I was a normal human, right?"

"Nah, it'll mean you were a human who was a bit dumber'n normal."

With that, Ladd raised his steel left hand. Even if all he did was let gravity take its course, he was sure to seriously hurt his opponent.

"Chris...!"

In an attempt to rescue Christopher, Rail took something out of her pocket, and Jacuzzi screamed, "N-no, Rail, you can't!"

Meanwhile, Graham spoke up in protest, swinging his wrench around. "Hey, Ladd, I mean it, quit! He's mine! If you swipe him, it'll be way more than just a sad story, and I'll have to wreck all the slots in this place!"

Why exactly?! Even as he yelled inwardly, Firo was already running to stop Ladd.

As he ran, he noticed something.

Christopher wasn't just taking a one-sided beating. Although his arm hung limply, his hand was gripping a fragment of the roulette table, one that was as sharp as a stake. He was probably planning to use the momentum of that downward blow to counterattack and run that fragment into Ladd.

No matter who won, in another moment, tragedy was going to erupt.

This was his gambling den, and there was no way in hell he'd let that happen between two people who called him a friend, even in a twisted way! Firo sprinted, preparing to get in the middle of that worst of all possible combinations and take both attacks himself, but then—

There was a noise.

A grand ensemble of bells echoed through the casino, stopping time for everyone at once.

Huh?

Firo knew what that sound was. He'd just heard it a few minutes earlier.

It was the unmistakable sound of someone hitting a jackpot on the casino's new slot machines.

What kind of astronomical odds would it take to hit two of those in a row?

Actually, forget that: Who was playing the slots while all this was going down?

Firo wasn't the only one confused. Nearly everyone who was still in the casino looked toward the sound, their minds filling up with questions.

Two men were standing at the right end of the row of seven slot machines.

One of them had features that put him somewhere between boyhood and late adolescence. He seemed to be about the same age as Firo.

As he looked at the man, Firo abruptly thought, *Oh. I know that face.*

He'd caught a glimpse of it in the casino today, too, but he'd skimmed right over it, since it hadn't registered as a new face for him.

No... Wait.

Yes, I do remember him.

But... This is... Huh? He's not one of the casino's big customers... is he...?

When he'd seen the man in a crowd of gamblers, he'd overlooked him. Now that he was looking at the boy alone, though, something tugged at Firo's heart.

The memory of that face seemed to linger in the deepest part of his mind.

Who is he...? Who is this guy?

As Firo considered this, his eyes went to the other man. That one was a dull-looking individual with Coke-bottle glasses. His hat was pulled down low, leaving his face in deep shadow. Between that and the whiskers around his mouth, it was impossible to tell the man's age.

And who's this guy? I've never seen him before. How long has he been in the casino?

A man with whiskers that striking should have stuck in his memory at least a little. He stayed silent and motionless, and Firo didn't know what to make of him.

In contrast to the taciturn bespectacled man, the young man scanned Firo's group, then gave an easy smile. As the slot machine finished its performance, he slowly began to clap.

"Wonderful. You've put on a very interesting show here."

The young man had lightly referred to the bloodthirsty fight to the death as "a show." He was clearly abnormal, and even as Ladd smiled, his temples twitched slightly. "Who're you, bastard?" he asked.

Bowing as respectfully as a butler, the young man introduced himself to everyone in the casino, Ladd included. "Pardon me. My name is Melvi."

"Melvi? That's one wacky name. If you enjoyed the show, you better be prepared to pay up."

"Pay? Pay, hmm…? Will this do, then?"

Melvi reached toward the slot machine's payout window, catching a few of the coins that were jingling out of it.

"Nah, not enough. I ain't cheap. You can't fudge it with that."

When he heard that, Graham gasped, then turned to Shaft and Lua, who'd come downstairs. "Not good… Shaft, Miz Lua, let me tell you an extremely not-good story. That Melvi fella… He's the type Ladd hates the most."

"…You're right," Lua murmured.

"Yeah…," Shaft agreed, clutching his head.

The people Ladd hated most were the type that didn't even consider the possibility that they might die. The type that got carried away, thinking their golden days would go on forever.

Despite the danger around him, the man didn't show the slightest trace of fear, nor did he seem prepared to die. He peppered Ladd with jokes, simply and calmly.

He was acting as if he was a god here.

What the man was doing was guaranteed to whip up Ladd's homicidal instincts. Shaft tried to figure out who he might be, but even Sham's knowledge held nothing about him.

Melvi gave a troubled smile. Then he took the cheapest type of token out of his pocket, fed it into the second slot machine from the right and, in an elegant motion, pulled the lever.

"?"

As Firo and the others frowned, the slot machine's reels spun vigorously. However, while they were still spinning, Melvi dropped a second token into the third machine from the right, then pulled its lever as well.

Depositing a coin in the middle slot machine, he pulled its lever, too. As he did, the first picture on the second machine from the right stopped on [7].

The moment he saw that, Firo felt horror crawl down his spine.

Hey, don't tell me...

As the fifth slot machine began to spin, the second reel on the second machine and the first reel on the third machine stopped, both on [7].

It can't be.

At that point, the others also figured out what was happening on the row of slot machines.

Once he'd set the sixth machine in motion, Melvi took a rather theatrical step, then gave another deep bow. He'd directed this one at Firo, not Ladd. That was when the third reel on the second machine from the right stopped, forming a perfect row of sevens.

The slot machine played its mechanical song of benediction.

A few seconds later, the third machine began the same melody, and then the fourth, so that a canon of slot machine music echoed in the casino.

Finally, the sixth machine from the right also produced triple sevens: Melvi had demonstrated a miracle.

Nader had won his initial jackpot on the machine on the far left. The machine on the far right was the one that had arrested Ladd and the others. In other words, the row of seven slots had all—on the same day, in the space of half an hour—turned out jackpots one after another.

Naturally, Firo understood: The only ones who'd call that a miracle were fools who never doubted anyone, messengers of God, or the very person who'd pulled off the cheat.

"You slimy piece of...," Firo grumbled.

Ladd wasn't the only one. Firo also decided this man was an enemy, and he glared at him, his temper growing sharper.

However, Melvi parried his glare with a friendly smile. In the midst of the slot machine ensemble, he spread his arms wide, as if to say he was the owner of the vast number of coins they'd ejected.

As the music stopped, he spoke politely to Firo. "I would have liked to see more of your show…but I thought, if I watched any longer, I wouldn't have time to greet you properly.

"In any case, it's almost time for my escort to arrive."

⟺

Outside the casino

"It's quiet now, so…I think we could probably go in…"

"Miss Annie, I really wouldn't. It's been incredibly noisy in there for a while."

Annie was trying to follow Ennis, and Czes was still encouraging her to stay back. Even Annie didn't seem sure whether she should go in. Every so often, she would mutter things like, "If I used someone stronger…" and "I can't afford to lose this body," but Czes's ears didn't catch half of it. He guessed she was probably frightened and confused about something, and he'd been trying to come up with ways to get her to wait outside.

He, Ennis, and Firo were immortal, so they'd be fine, but that wasn't true of Annie. Or at the very least, Czes wasn't aware that it was. Hence, he wanted her to act out her romantic rivalry with Ennis in some other, less dangerous direction.

After all, since he'd become an immortal while he was still a child, love affairs were foreign to him. As one of his few amusements, he wanted to watch Firo stuck in this tug-of-war.

Precisely because Czes was thinking like a small-time scoundrel, Annie was a valuable part of his entertainment; he didn't want to lose her.

…However, curses—like chickens—come home to roost.

As Czes attempted to relish the unhappiness of his neighbor and his woman troubles, he received a just reward.

In other words, he began to develop woman trouble of his own.

* * *

"Czes? ...That is you, isn't it, Czes?"

"Huh?"

Someone had called to him abruptly from behind, and he responded involuntarily.

A girl who seemed slightly older than Czes was standing there.

"Oh, thank goodness... I knew it was you!"

She must have been afraid she'd gotten the wrong person. The girl sounded a little timid, but she smiled at him, sighing with relief.

"...Mary?"

Without thinking, he said her name.

Mary Beriam, the daughter of Senator Beriam, was the girl who'd been taken hostage by the men in black suits during the Flying Pussyfoot incident.

Czes only pretended to be a child, and he'd tried to use her as camouflage by playing with her on the train. If she still remembered him now, more than three years later, apparently both he and the incident had made a deep impression on her.

By the time he realized he should have insisted she had the wrong person, it was too late. She took his hands and looked down at him. She was a little taller than he was.

"Huh? Czes, were you always shorter than me?"

It was an innocent, childlike question.

Breaking out in a cold sweat, Czes said the first thing that came into his head.

"I—I haven't hit my growth spurt yet. I'll get taller soon. It kind of bugs me, so could you not bring it up?"

"Oh! I—I'm sorry, Czes. I was just...so happy..."

Mary was as timid as she had been three years ago, but time had changed her, transforming her from a child younger than Czes to a girl in her early teens.

"But... Really, thank you so much for what you did for me on that train! If you hadn't given me courage, I...I might have died there..." Mary pulled Czes into a tight hug.

An ordinary boy would probably have blushed, but Czes went pale instead.

Oh, hell. If I'm friends with this girl, she'll eventually realize I'm immortal.

As fellow immortals, Firo's group didn't pose a problem, but if ordinary people found out about him, things would get hairy. He'd experienced that far too many times already. On top of that, this girl was a senator's daughter. If she told her father the immortals' secret and he happened to believe her, there was bound to be trouble.

But why now?!

As Mary hugged him, Czes began to curse his own fate. America was a big country, and naturally, it was no coincidence that Mary was here. The being who'd created the inevitability Czes wanted to curse spoke from behind the girl, and it wasn't God.

"Is that the boy who saved you on the train, Mary?"

When Czes looked toward the voice, he saw a boy about Mary's age, right at the beginning of his teens.

"Well, we'll go get Mr. Melvi, so you wait here, Mary. If we take you into a casino, your father will be furious."

The boy started down the stairs, followed by an entourage of several other people. As he looked at that group, Czes realized what position the boy occupied. Even as the situation bewildered him, the face of his roommate rose in his mind.

Firo... What in the world did you do?

⇔

Inside the casino

"Whoops, speak of the devil. Here they come," Melvi murmured, turning toward the stairs.

The employee who'd come tumbling down those stairs had already been helped by other staff members, who'd carried him into the office.

Everyone who was still in the casino followed Melvi's gaze to the empty stairs and heard several pairs of footsteps, coming down.

The first person to appear was a young man in a formal swallowtail coat. He wore a pair of goggles on his forehead. Between those and the gloves on both of his hands, he seemed to be a biker.

A biker in a swallowtail coat struck them as odd, but several of the others who followed him down seemed out of place in a casino as well. The most striking one was a boy who seemed to be a few years older than Czes and Rail, no more than Ricardo's age. He was smiling ingenuously. Behind him came several beautiful women who wore faint smiles and chic dresses of black and white. Tall, muscular men in black suits formed a protective perimeter around them—And finally, a man with the exact same features and clothes as the first man descended the stairs as the group's rearguard.

The boy, who was guarded front and rear by a set of twins in swallowtail coats, smiled and began waving as soon as he saw Melvi. The reaction was terribly unsophisticated. It intensified the impression his black clothes gave, and Firo, who was steeped in the criminal underworld, felt an indescribable eeriness about him.

It wasn't that he sensed malice behind it; it was just that the kid's straightforward innocence felt wrong somehow.

In contrast to the boy, Melvi wore his smile like a mask. He went up to the group that stood at the foot of the stairs. "Well, well. Young Master Carzelio. To think you'd come in person."

"I keep telling you to call me Cazze."

"No, no, I'm here to deliver a formal greeting. I can't call you by your nickname."

A greeting? Overhearing the pair's exchange, Firo frowned. *Come to think of it, he did say something like that earlier.*

As if he'd read Firo's mind, Melvi turned back to face him. With an exaggerated gesture, he said, "All right, once again, it's a pleasure to make your acquaintance, Mr. Firo Prochainezo. My name is Melvi. I will be serving as the dealer for the Runoratas' room, in the casino which that family is about to open."

Melvi bowed politely. From behind him, Carzelio spoke to Firo, his childlike eyes shining even more brightly. "So you're Firo from the Martillos?! I've heard about you! Thank you very much for being part of my grandfather's event!"

"Your grandfather?"

"Oh! ...I'm sorry. I hadn't introduced myself! I'm Carzelio Runorata!"

The moment the boy gave his name, Firo stiffened again.

Someone with blood ties to the Runoratas, huh? I knew it.

Firo's cheeks were drawn and tense, while Carzelio smiled at him cheerfully. "I'll only be there as a guest, but I'm really looking forward to seeing what kind of betting your group does!"

"...No, we're honored to have been invited," Firo told him, although the courtesy was empty. Forcing a smile, he turned to Melvi. "Then all that earlier stuff was part of your 'greeting'?"

Melvi shrugged. "A grifter, an unnatural jackpot, a thug with a gun. I was looking forward to seeing how you'd handle it, and it was quite exhilarating. You appear to have a lot of fascinating friends. That last fight... That unforeseen complication was a sight to behold, but I feared I was going to run out of time, so I took the liberty of stopping it."

"......!"

According to Melvi, everything—all the way back to the card sharp—had been a setup.

Firo thought he might be bluffing, but then again, he might be telling the truth. Even if the latter was true, Melvi probably hadn't told the cheater what he was really after. He'd just egged him on by telling him something else. As far as Firo was concerned, even that made the man a hopeless lowlife.

Dammit... I knew it. He does look like somebody. He's the spitting image of...

Of who? Who does he look like?

I've seen him. I've seen this guy before...

The murky thoughts that welled up inside him got in the way, and Firo couldn't quite focus all his hostility on him.

However, someone else certainly could; he smiled with consummate malice at Melvi.

"I see, I see... Yeah, I get it... It all makes sense now. I get it all the way down, right to the bottom." Ladd Russo chuckled as if he was enjoying himself. In a slow, menacing motion, he turned to face Melvi. "The Runorata Family, huh? Well, ain't that something. You're one of the biggest outfits out here."

"Melvi, who is that man?" Carzelio asked.

Melvi smiled. "A murderer, just a maniac. There's nothing to worry about, Master Carzelio."

"A murderer?! Wow! I've never seen one of those before!"

Unlike when he'd spoken to Firo, Carzelio sounded like a genuine child, and his eyes sparkled. Everyone else found it disturbing.

Taking the boy's rather unhinged words at face value, Ladd joined the conversation on the same frequency. "Oho. So it's your first time seeing a homicidal maniac, huh? Well, today's your lucky day, kid. And hey, pretty soon, you just might get to see this very same maniac butcher somebody."

Ladd rolled his left shoulder lightly, then asked Melvi a question, without bothering to hide his hostility. "So is that what this is? Is that what you're thinking? You're connected to the Runorata Family, so if you speak up and say so, there ain't nobody who'd lay a finger on you?"

"Yes. Anyone who did would be a fool, wouldn't they?" Melvi said bluntly, and he smiled.

Ladd already knew it—even now, when he was faced with a bloodthirsty killer, Melvi didn't have any fear that he might die here.

"So is that it? You think there couldn't possibly be any fools like that around here? Basically, you think there's no way you could die… Ain't that right?"

"Well, of course." Still smiling, Melvi spoke with assurance, as if he was intentionally goading him. "Certainly not because of you."

"So you mean to say that— Die."

Right in the middle of his sentence, as he paused for breath—Ladd was already in motion.

Closing several feet, he expertly shifted his center of gravity and brought his prosthetic hand down on him diagonally, at maximum force. If that attack hit home, the man's upper half would splatter like a tomato hit by a baseball bat before he even had time for regret.

*   *   *

And yet, Melvi didn't even try to dodge.

Just before the blow fell, the bearded man with glasses cut in from the side, caught Ladd's arm with one hand—and, in an economical motion, *broke down* Ladd's center of gravity.

"...Hunh?"

Although Ladd didn't understand what had happened, the momentum of his lethal attack was stolen away, then converted into a throw and used against him. He spun, flying off to the side behind Melvi, where he crashed into the casino wall.

"Gah...!"

"Ladd!" Graham was startled, but Ladd got up as though nothing had happened. Smiling, he glared at the man who'd gotten in his way.

"Whoa, ow-ow-ow... So what are you butting in for, Whisker-Specs?"

Ladd hit the bearded man with the same intent to kill he'd turned on Melvi, but the man didn't respond. He just stood in front of Ladd, barring his way, guarding Melvi.

Meanwhile, that maneuver had shocked Firo in a different way.

"...Wow."

It was probably something similar to the martial arts he'd learned from Yaguruma... But could he have diverted the speed and force of Ladd's attack? No matter how much he trained, he'd probably have to be on Yaguruma's level before he could do that in the middle of an actual fight.

That guy is genuinely bad news. Is he a Runorata man? Who the hell is he...?

A fella like that... You'd have to be Ronny to— He glanced at Ronny, who was in a corner of the casino, then hastily forced himself to focus. *Look, come on, don't lean on Ronny!*

Even as Firo scolded himself, Ladd was closing in on the bearded man, smiling with every step. Then, with even greater speed than earlier, he paid out several high-speed jabs, skimming through a repeating pattern of small steps.

However, evading them all with the slippery flexibility of a willow, the man set the heel of his palm against Ladd's chest. It looked as if he'd only touched him lightly, but Ladd's upper body snapped backward, and he crashed to the ground.

As he watched the man twist Ladd around his little finger, Firo's mouth hung open.

Suddenly, Luck, who'd emerged from the office somewhere in there, called to him. "Firo."

"Huh? Hey, Luck! Check this guy out. He's incredible!"

Firo was all worked up, but Luck responded coldly. "I wonder where he learned that sort of thing. He *did* say he'd been into martial arts recently."

Firo made an incredulous nose. "Huh?" Luck was talking as if he knew the man.

"...You mean you haven't caught on?" Luck asked, startled by Firo's reaction. Then, raising his voice slightly, he called to the man with the beard. "You're wearing that disguise *again*? Are you partial to it or something?"

The bearded, bespectacled man shot a glance at Luck.

"The glasses are different and so's the color of the beard... How'd you know? Man, count on you to notice, Luck."

The sound of that voice sent a shock through Firo. "Huh... Wait, what?!"

The voice that issued from that mountainous beard was one Firo knew.

"The hair that shows under your hat doesn't match the beard at all. You should dye them the same color, at least."

"Oh yeah. Good point. I can't do that, though. It's just not gonna happen, Luck." With a glance at Ladd, who was back on his feet, the bearded man spoke sadly.

Then he stripped off his hat, false beard, and glasses.

"The thing is, Chané said my hair was pretty."

* * *

“““““““?!”””””””

At the sight of the face he’d revealed, five people—Firo, Jacuzzi, Christopher, Ladd, and Graham—found themselves speechless at the exact same time.

There was no telling where his previous quiet energy had gone. Now that he’d shown himself, the redheaded man casually raised a hand as if he was a regular young guy, the kind you could find anywhere in town.

“Hey, Firo.”

“Fuh… Felix?!”

“Oho, you’re finally calling me Felix on instinct, instead of Claire! Good, fantastic! Claire’s dead. Now I live only in my girl’s heart.”

“No, hang on, hold it! What’s going on here?! Explain all this, Felix!”

Felix Walken, formerly known as Claire Stanfield—originally a hitman nicknamed Vino, he’d faked his own death on the Flying Pussyfoot, began using the name of Felix “the Handyman,” and embarked on a new life.

Due to his unparalleled physical abilities and strong will, he was often called things like genius, monster, and the ultimate hitman. On Firo’s list of people he never wanted to make an enemy of, he was right up there with Ronny. That said, he’d been a friend of Firo’s since they were kids, and the guy was a sworn ally to the Gandor brothers as well.

“Explain, huh? Well, uh, it won’t take much explaining.” At that, Felix looked away just a little awkwardly—

Then, smiling, he hit Firo with the news, point-blank.

“Sorry, Firo. I’m not on your team this time.”

⇔

Somewhere in New York Chané’s hideout

“By the way, Chané. I hear you have a lover.”

In the apartment, Chané’s moving reunion was still underway.

Chané, now dressed, flinched at her father's words.

I knew it. Father knows everything. I could never keep a secret from him.

She was certain of this, but at the same time, she grew uneasy. It was an unease her old self had never felt. She couldn't really put a name to it. She clenched her fists lightly, waiting to hear what her father would say next.

The words that came out of his mouth were not the ones she had expected at all.

"He's quite an interesting fellow, isn't he?"

"......?"

From the way her father spoke, it sounded almost as if they'd met already. Chané cocked her head, puzzled.

As if answering her question, Huey gave a thin smile.

"Before coming to see you, I met and spoke with him briefly...and made *a bit of a contract* with him."

⇔

Inside the casino

"See, I made *a bit of a contract* with my girl's old man. I'm the body-guard for that snotty punk Melvi over there."

As Felix bluntly called the person he was supposed to guard "snotty," Melvi shrugged and grinned sarcastically.

"I didn't want to square up against you guys, so I wore a disguise and hoped you wouldn't figure it out. But then you went and saw right through it, Luck."

"Wait, just... Hold it, about—everything."

"Oh, I really am just a bodyguard, so rest easy there. If he'd told me to crush or bump off the Martillos and the Gandors, I mean, even if it was my girl's old man who was asking... You know?"

Firo didn't understand at all, and he pressed his old friend for answers. "No, I don't know! Don't give me that! What's this contract?!"

* * *

"Hey..."

A voice spoke from another direction. The emotions in it were as hot as compressed magma, and Firo tensed up.

"You... I remember you, bastard... Your voice, that red hair, those joker eyes... Yeah, like I'd ever forget!"

The voice belonged to Ladd. The feelings that had begun to churn inside him when he saw Felix were joy, rage, nostalgia—and an overwhelming urge to murder him.

"What is this...?" *(Kill, kill, kill, kill...)* "Is this casino actually Neverland or something?" *(Kill, kill, kill, kill, kill, kill, kill, kill, kill, kill...)* "How come all these old pals and buddies and people I want to slaughter keep turning up?" *(Kill, kill...)*

His glaring eyes, the breath he exhaled as he spoke, every tiny gesture—it all exuded a boiling, savage intent, to the point that no matter what Ladd actually said, it sounded as if he was actually muttering the word *kill*.

Although Ladd was obviously not acting normal, the redheaded Handyman spoke to him in a friendly tone. "Hey there. You survived, huh? Glad to see your girl's doing well, too."

When Felix shot a glance at Lua, she paled. Those words seemed to have tipped her off as well: This redhead was the red monster she'd once encountered on the roof of a train.

"Sorry about using you as a threat that time. But y'know, since you fell for a homicidal maniac, you're probably prepared for ugly stuff to happen to you, right?"

Luck looked from Felix, who was smiling, to the frightened woman. "I don't know the circumstances here, but I suspect you did something awful to this woman. You owe her a better apology."

"What?! Luck, c'mon! What kind of problem kid do you think I am?" Felix refuted the idea in a lackadaisical tone, but he knew Luck had a point. "...That said, uh, maybe so. Should I apologize more sincerely or something?"

While Felix was casually asking Luck for advice—

*   *   *

—Ladd hurled half of the broken roulette table at him.

As his bloodlust soared to new heights, the adrenaline seemed to have boosted his strength. Ignoring the screams of the muscles in his right arm, he pitched a chunk of roulette table that had to weigh over forty pounds as if it were a baseball.

Felix knocked it out of the air with a heel drop, using the kickback to launch himself into the air.

Just then, another face closed in, right in front of him. It was Christopher, who also had a bone to pick with him. Launching himself off a nearby baccarat table, he tried to hit the airborne Felix with a spin kick, but using Christopher's outstretched leg as a steppingstone, Felix jumped even higher.

The ceiling wasn't all that high. Grabbing the chandelier, he swung from it like a pendulum, then used his momentum to execute a midair jump, as if he were on a flying trapeze at the circus.

Then he kicked the approaching wall, bouncing off it and toward Ladd.

Christopher tried to break in from the side and counterstrike, but Graham attacked him with his giant wrench. "That's my brother Ladd's mark! If you get in the way, I'll turn you into a sad story they'll tell down through the ages!"

"Look, seriously, you're the one who's in the way!"

As they clashed again, beside them, Ladd picked up the other half of the roulette table, swinging it at Felix.

Before long, that violence pulled in both Christopher and Graham, and they rampaged around the casino like a mini tornado.

"Agh, no, you shouldn't fight!" Carzelio scolded them, as if he were reprimanding naughty little kids. Jacuzzi and the others stared at him, thinking that he really couldn't be quite right in the head.

Meanwhile, a pale-faced Firo yelled desperately at the core of the violence.

"Wait— Don't— Knock it off, fellas! Enough already!"

"I think you should probably evacuate your employees," Luck said calmly.

Firo signaled his staff with a glance. "You too, Ennis. For now, take those kids and get outside..." As he spoke, he spotted a man on the stairs, scrambling to get out the door. It was the guy who'd said Ladd had told him about this place. The one who'd touched off this riot.

What, he's making a run for it?!

He instinctively yelled, trying to stop him, but—

"Oh, he doesn't matter. That man's scum. Just let him be." Melvi spoke in a quiet voice; he'd come up right beside Firo.

"...?! Why, you— When did you...?!" Firo snapped at him, not bothering to feign civility.

Putting his face up close to Firo's, Melvi whispered in his ear, taunting him. "Your true colors are showing. That's no good. Dealers should always wear a poker face."

"I'm just the manager. I'm not a dealer." Listening to the sound of a roulette table being smashed up nearby, Firo narrowed his eyes. "If you weren't with the Runoratas, I'd be rolling you up in a rug and dumping you in the Hudson right about now."

"You do say some frightening things. Have I ever done anything to wrong you?"

"Nope. I'll do you a favor and take the blame for today, since I was the idiot who didn't see it coming... But I'm sure now. You're a psycho. And I'm sure you've got something up your sleeve for that gambling meet."

Firo was trying to gauge the other man's real ability, and he wasn't being the least bit careless. However, he genuinely had seen the young man's face somewhere before, and the slight confusion unsettled him.

Dammit, who is he? Where have I seen this guy...?

Meanwhile, Melvi smiled and continued on, unperturbed. "You and I have become friends, after all. Why don't we play a little game on the day?"

"...There, see? You're planning to swipe something from us, aren't you? What is it? Territory? Money?"

Firo snorted, but Melvi's eyes narrowed. Leaning in even closer to Firo, he whispered in a voice only he could hear.

"What I want…is Szilard Quates's knowledge. That's all."

"—?!" Firo tensed.

At the same time, still smiling, Melvi bit through his own lip.

A little blood trickled out of the corner of his mouth, and a few seconds later, the blood began to writhe as if it had a will of its own, returning to the wound on his lip…until at last, even the wound was gone.

"……!"

Firo stared in silence, his eyes wide.

"I hope we have a chip that's worth enough to balance the wager, but…"

Wearing the same masklike smile he'd worn a moment ago, Melvi spoke as if nothing had happened.

"I anticipate our match will be a good one, Firo Prochainezo."

⟺

Outside the casino

Hurry! I've gotta get outta here, fast!

Dammit, what are those monsters?

And the Runorata Family, too…? I ain't gonna stick around for that!

Nader stripped off his suit jacket, leaving himself in his button-down shirt. He hit the top of the stairs just as he was tying the bundles of bills up in the jacket.

But…is this okay?

Abruptly, the promise he'd made when he was young flickered through his heart.

Isn't this my chance to make a change?

Something deep inside Nader was trying to keep him there.

Right now, this was definitely no place for normal people. But what if that meant he'd get a chance to stop being normal here?

Hesitating, Nader stopped in his tracks.

Right in front of him, some young children were talking. The scenery was peaceful. As he took it in, that promise came back to him more vividly.

Be a hero...

No, but... What am I supposed to do there?

If he gave back the money, at least, would he stop feeling as if he was in their debt? With that thought in mind, Nader hesitantly started to turn around. Facing him down was a girl in her late teens, glaring at him.

"......?" He didn't recognize her. He'd taken his jacket off; did she think that was weird?

As Nader wondered about that, the girl quietly approached him. Then she spoke in a hate-filled voice only he could hear.

"Nader Schasschule... Why are you here, hmm?"

With a shudder, he felt all his blood retreat into his depths, while a cold sweat broke out all over his skin. He didn't recognize the girl's voice, but that sticky tone of hers was familiar. It really didn't match her appearance.

"Were you sneaking around during the Chicago incident as well?" she asked.

"......"

He had no memory of any "Chicago incident," but he couldn't even argue. He'd tensed up so fast he could hear all his joints creak.

As if matching the rhythm of those strange noises, the girl gave her name. There was a sharp light in her eyes.

"We...Hilton...*will never forgive traitors.*"

"Agh... AAAAAAaaaaaAAAaaAaaAAAH!"

With a scream that was pretty far from anyone's idea of a hero, Nader took to his heels.

He didn't have the mental capacity to feel conflicted anymore. He just followed his instincts and ran.

At this point, running was all he could do.

As he watched the man sprint away from the casino, another man who'd just arrived adjusted his glasses and frowned. "...What on earth was that? Has there actually been some sort of trouble here?"

The man who headed for the casino's entrance, walking a little faster, was Maiza Avaro, the Martillo Family's treasurer.

A client who'd just happened to run past him on the street had told him "Some guy's knocking over your casino!" and so he'd hurried over to check on things.

Spotting Czes and Annie near the casino's entrance, Maiza called to them, although he didn't stop.

"Are you two all right? I heard they'd had trouble here."

"Oh...Maiza." Czes, who was standing next to a girl Maiza didn't recognize, looked startled.

"We don't really know, but there's been an incredible racket down there..." Annie's face had already returned to normal.

When Maiza heard that, all he said was, "You three get away from here and take shelter in another building *immediately*." Then he started rapidly down the stairs.

He had no idea what he was about to see down there.

⟺

A few minutes earlier   Inside the casino

"Felix, I'm leaving now. Stop playing around, would you?" Melvi said, turning his back on Firo.

When he heard him, Claire launched himself off the floor, instantly putting distance between himself and the other three.

Several casino tables had been broken, and three of the chandeliers were on the floor.

Firo was kind of amazed they'd managed to do so much damage in the minute or so he'd spent talking to Melvi, but at this point he didn't have the presence of mind to be shocked, or the time to clutch his head in anguish.

He's...an immortal?

And Felix is his bodyguard?

That meant Firo had no chance of making like a gangster and doing something about the guy in an ambush.

"Hey... Hold up. We're not done yet." Panting, Ladd set his hands on the edge of an as-yet-unharmed baccarat table and squeezed, making it creak audibly. If left to himself, he would probably pick up the table one-handed.

Graham and Christopher were also watching Felix closely. As one would expect from people who'd just inflicted horrendous violence on each other, they were out of breath, and their foreheads were sweaty.

Although he'd been in the thick of it all, Felix Walken wasn't even breathing hard, and there wasn't a single drop of sweat on his sleeves. "Would you fellas hurry up and learn you can't beat me already? Whaddaya mean, 'We're not done yet'? Don't get the wrong idea. We never even started."

Felix had composure to spare, and he wasn't through goading Ladd and the others. With a bored sigh, he turned his back on them. "If you've got beef with me, bring it anytime. Feel free to come at me with as many friends as you want. Try to give me a little challenge."

When he'd said that much, he stopped dead, then looked back and went on. "We were at Firo's casino today, though, so I made sure nobody bled on it."

The expression on his face belonged to an endlessly callous killer—that of Vino.

Jacuzzi, who'd been careless enough to look, felt his consciousness start to drift out of reach. Rail broke out in a cold sweat, her expression tense.

Any ordinary person would have been petrified, even if they'd only glimpsed his eyes, but Ladd's urge to kill swelled even further—and he laughed. "Ha-ha... Ha-ha-ha-ha-ha-ha-ha-ha! Haw-ha-ha-

ha-ha-ha-ha-ha-ha! 'Bring it anytime,' huh? ...Yeah! That's a good one! That's exactly what laid-back lugs who think they won't die always say! Yeah, yeah, yeah! I'll do that for you any day, buddy!"

His laughter stopped abruptly, and he actually did pick up the baccarat table with one hand. "In that case, heck... It's fine if I go now, ain't it, Rail Tracer...!"

However, Ladd saw something that stopped him in his tracks.

At some point during the exchange, Melvi had taken a handgun from his jacket, and he was pointing it at Lua.

"......!"

Instantly, some of the ferocity he'd focused on Felix was diverted to Melvi.

Letting the enormous malice flow past him as if it were a cool breeze, Melvi put his gun away, still smiling. "You take my meaning, don't you? Let that be enough for today."

Melvi tilted his head, his lips curving. Ladd clenched his fist, tightly. He squeezed so hard his fingernails split the skin on his palm, and blood trickled out. "Listen up. There are two guys I swore I'd kill once I was out of the big house. One's the ginger over there, and the other's Huey Laforet." Ladd's voice was brimming over with rage. Several people reacted to the name "Huey"—and in particular, Rail's expression changed conspicuously.

"You said your name was Melvi, yeah? ...You're the third guy on that list," Ladd spat, looking at the floor. Nobody around him could see his eyes, but the *vicious* grin they saw on his lips made the air in the casino as sharp as ice.

For just a moment, Melvi's expression nearly vanished. However, he promptly recovered his smile. "...Do as you please. If you *can* kill me, that is," he said, starting toward the stairs.

Felix went next, and Carzelio was about to follow him when he seemed to realize something. His eyes widened in surprise, and he hastily turned back to Firo. "I'm sorry our dealer's bodyguard got into a fight and broke your casino. If you bill us for the repair fees and your losses, the Runorata Family will guarantee as much of it as we can. I promise."

Carzelio's eyes were honest. He probably meant exactly what he said, but it made Firo feel as if he was being challenged in another way.

It took everything he had to respond. "…Well, thanks. I'm grateful for your generosity, kid."

When Melvi came up beside Ronny, his steps slowed, and he whispered with a thin smile. "What's between Firo and myself is just a spat between immortals. I have no intention of opposing the Martillos, so be at ease, Ronny."

Melvi spoke as if he knew what Ronny really was. The Martillo Family's secretary responded impassively. "I'm not so sure about that. Going after Firo is the same as firing on our family, but… Well, never mind."

Without saying another word, Ronny watched the Runorata group go.

Then, just as Melvi stepped onto the stairs that led up to ground level, a belated visitor appeared.

A tall, bespectacled man looked in from the top of the stairs. Almost immediately, he saw Firo in the center of the casino and the wretched condition of the place. "Firo! Are you all right? What is…? What in the world…?" Maiza descended quickly.

Just as he reached the last step…he froze, staring at Melvi's face.

"…Excuse me." With a nod to Maiza, Melvi passed him, leading his entourage back above ground.

Stiffly, Maiza tried to keep watching Melvi, but other people came between them, and then he couldn't see him anymore.

After they were gone, Maiza murmured just one word. His eyes looked as if he'd seen a ghost.

"…Gretto…?"

As soon as Firo heard that name, something clicked deep inside him.

He could almost hear it, like the sound of a lock being opened.

And in fact, a lock had been forced open in the depths of his heart,

and a memory that ordinarily stayed out of sight had begun rampaging through his mind.

Gretto.

Gretto Avaro.

He was Maiza's kid brother, a fledgling alchemist who'd been eaten by Szilard Quates.

In other words, Gretto's memories had been inside Szilard's memories, which meant they were still dormant in Firo.

I see...

At that point, Firo finally remembered, realizing why Melvi had looked familiar.

When Szilard Quates ate people he hadn't known for long, he never really remembered what they looked like. The familiarity had come from Gretto's own memories.

In other words, that guy Melvi—

He was identical to *Gretto's own reflection in a mirror*—the one Gretto himself knew.

⇔

Outside the casino

"Huh? Czes? Where could he have gone...?"

Mary looked around, mystified. However, the moment Felix had emerged from downstairs, Czes had bolted without even taking time to scream. On top of that, the woman who'd been with him had vanished somewhere along the way. Mary tilted her head in confusion, a little dazed.

"Sorry to keep you waiting, Mary," Carzelio said. "I'll take you home, then."

"Huh...? Oh, yes. Thank you, Cazze!"

"It's fine. I have to give the letter my grandfather sent with me to Mr. Beriam anyway."

With that, Carzelio showed Mary to the car.

* * *

As if taking the children's place, a man who'd been standing beside the car slowly walked up to Melvi. "To think you'd make your subordinates pull a stunt like *that* just so you could introduce yourself to the enemy. What are you trying to do here?"

The man wore glasses, and he had a cloth tied over his shaved head. From the fact that the twin bodyguards weren't moving, he seemed to be an acquaintance.

"Don't look so upset, Tim." Melvi laughed.

Tim's expression turned sour. "...Are you even a little conscious that you're *the leader* of Time? There's no way you don't know just how big the current experiment is."

"Have no fear. I'll do everything I've been told, and nothing that's forbidden. In all else, I'm free. Isn't that right? It's true of me, and those of you in Larva, and Rhythm, and Sham and Hilton, too." Melvi grinned.

Realizing it was pointless to say anything else to him, Tim's face went blank, and he replied tersely. "I hate your guts. The sooner you get that through your head, the better."

"Please don't let it bother you. I can't stand you, either."

Starting toward his car, Melvi added one final comment.

"I obey the will of my master. That's all."

Interlude The Police Can't Move

Inside the casino

"Let me tell you a sad, sad story."

In the casino, where everyone was silent, Graham was the first one to speak.

"I didn't know what to do back there. Should I team up with my man Ladd and take that Felix fella down?! Or should I respect his one-on-one fight and focus on taking apart the red-eyed bastard who was trying to get in the way?! And! The result! Of that! Hesitation! Is! This! Hell!"

As Graham yelled, he was swinging his wrench around rhythmically. His eyes were on the smashed-up game tables and the fallen, crushed frames of the chandeliers.

"This is just destruction! It's not demolition! Nothing about this feels good. What now, Shaft?! What should I do?! How can I atone for my crimes and make everything broken go back to normal so it can get demolished properly and bring about world peace?!"

"Forget that. Just shut up, please."

"...It's fine. Let 'im scream, Shaft." Hearing Graham yell the way he always did seemed to have calmed Ladd down a bit. He cracked his neck in a show of boredom, then spoke to Firo. "I'll foot the bill for your busted casino. No sense in letting the Runoratas do you any favors." Smacking his prosthetic left hand into his right palm, he muttered, half to himself. "I've got nothing to do with the Martillo Family, so I'll slaughter that shithead Melvi for you. That'll cover it, right?"

Firo seemed to be trying to organize the various doubts he'd developed. He just stood in the center of the casino, silently, and didn't respond to Ladd. Ennis was watching him from a distance, and Ronny didn't seem particularly inclined to give him advice, either.

Christopher started to speak to Firo, but Ricardo grabbed his arm, pulling him back. "I think you should wait until he's calmed down, Christopher."

"Really? I'm a pragmatist, you see. I'd like to ask him about that Felix fellow's weak points now..."

"Yeah, um, Chris, I really don't think you should do that just yet." Even Rail discouraged him, and Christopher shrugged, moving away from Firo.

Jacuzzi, who'd nearly passed out from the sheer impact of Vino, had been gazing at them in a daze. However, he suddenly realized something and spoke up. "N-never mind that, shouldn't we get out of the casino, fast...? It's been a while since those first gunshots, and then there was a whole lot of noise a minute ago, so the police are probably just about here, right...?"

Maiza, who'd been thinking until just then, abruptly raised his head and reassured Jacuzzi. "*No*, I don't think the police will be coming."

"Huh...? What do you mean, Maiza?" Firo asked now that the sound of Maiza's voice put him more at ease.

"Well... There's a huge commotion about it on the radio, but it doesn't sound as though any have flown this way."

"Flown...? What's flying?" Firo looked even more perplexed.

As Maiza filled him in, he wore a complicated expression.

"Right now, sites throughout Manhattan are under attack by strange aircraft, and the police are tied up dealing with them."

⇔

All over New York City

In Manhattan, the sun had set, and night had come.

The dim light of neon signs dominated the dark sky. The seaplanes, which had appeared in that sky, flew between buildings or high over parks and broad avenues, sending the drone of their engines echoing all throughout town.

On top of that, the machine guns that were fixed to their noses were spitting sparks, scattering heavy, unmistakable reports of gun violence across the city.

"Eeeeeeeeeeeep?! V-Vice President! It's a war! It's all over for us! I was a lousy apprentice, and I never managed to get a full score, but I'm really glad I was able to be apprenticed to you, Vice President! Waaaaaaaaaaaaaaaaaah!"

Carol, who'd encountered one of those planes on a street corner, panicked and clung to her boss's leg. However, the boss in question—Gustav St. Germain, vice president of the *Daily Days* newspaper—calmly observed the seaplane, then gently patted Carol's head.

"Calm yourself, Carol… I hear shots, but no sounds of impact. Those are most likely blanks."

⟺

New York Inside the Gandor Family office

"……"

"Hey, Keith, what the hell is going on out there?"

Under a jazz hall, in the office of the Gandor Family, Keith and Berga were playing a game of poker with some of their men. Just then, Tick and Maria, who'd gone to see what was happening outside, came downstairs.

"Umm, there were airplanes flying around. Airplanes are really keeeeen, huh."

"It's incredible, amigo! They were flying really low, between the buildings! If I jumped from the third floor or so, I just know I could cut 'em! Actually, do you think it would be okay if I did that, amigo?!"

The pair's extremely scattered report made Berga scowl, but Keith just drew a card, his face as expressionless as ever. Then, when he looked at the number he'd pulled, his face clouded over slightly.

"......"

"Hunh? Keith, how'd that happen? Pulling a card like that from a deck that's ninety percent jokers..."

As he gazed at the "7" card he'd set on the table, Keith felt a strange unease. Getting up, he went outside to take a look for himself.

He felt an overwhelming premonition that, before they knew it, they'd gotten dragged into some vast scheme—and he was steeling himself to smash it to pieces.

⇔

Somewhere in New York Victor's investigation headquarters

"Now you've done it, damn you... You finally pulled the trigger, huh, Huey!"

Listening to the noise of the engines as they passed over the investigation headquarters, Victor slammed a fist into his desk.

"Dammit! Those airplanes—well, technically seaplanes—they're shooting blanks! They're just a distraction! Tell the men to focus on the ground! He's planning to pull something big while the cops are tied up with this, and you can take that to the bank!"

He was half right.

At this point in time, the seaplanes were no more than a distraction.

However, there was something Victor hadn't realized yet: Melvi had set this up so he could greet Firo without police interference, and it had nothing to do with Huey's experiment.

In addition, the seaplanes that were currently wreaking havoc were only a fraction of the aircraft held by Time, which Huey had on standby out on the Atlantic.

⇔

Somewhere in New York

"Teacher, there's a whole lot of noise out there. Is the house going to be okay?"

The speaker was a boy whose face wasn't quite out of childhood.

The man who responded was doing maintenance on a large quantity of guns. "Let it be, Apprentice One. I can tell from the sound. Those are blanks."

With his eyes fixed on the countless gleaming gun components, the man—Smith—went on calmly. "Never mind that. Graham went to pick up that Ladd fellow, and it's about time for him to get home… Ladd, Ladd, Ladd. That rotten murderer is another ludicrous fool who, like me, is possessed by the flower of insanity. The lunatic bloom that graces him attracts only poisonous insects, though. That's because he has no sense of aesthetics. On that point, my—"

The rest of his sentence was completely drowned out by an airplane that flew right past the building.

Interrupted, Smith clicked his tongue and muttered:

"Rgh…! Bunch of uncultured louts."

⟺

Chané's hideout

"Oho…" After hearing a report one of his subordinates had stopped by to deliver, Huey turned to Chané, who was gazing out the window. "Chané, it sounds as though Hilton, the spy, has located an old friend of ours."

"?"

An old friend? Could it be Spike?

That traitor.

I didn't trust him to begin with, and if he's Father's enemy, I'll dispose of—

That was what Chané thought, but… The name she actually heard was one she'd just been thinking of a few moments ago and had never expected to hear at a time like this.

"Nader Schasschule."

"?!"

"The man who once betrayed the Lemures. The one whose right hand you cut off. He's alive, here in town."

As Huey relayed that information, he seemed rather entertained. He wasn't trying to manipulate his daughter. From his expression, he was simply looking forward to seeing what Chané would do once she knew about this.

Under her father's gaze, Chané lowered her eyes and thought.

I see.

That was when my gears slipped—because I didn't properly dispose of Nader.

However, that had nothing to do with anything now… And yet, in the depths of her heart, Chané had made up her mind.

If she wanted to regain her former sharp edge—she probably needed to kill Nader.

If I find him here in town, I won't fail to cut him down this time.
I'll do it without feeling a thing. As if I'm taking out the trash.

⇔

Somewhere in New York

"What the hell…? What's going on here?!"

As he looked up at the airplanes flying every which way, Nader kept on running, with no destination in mind.

When they let him out of the pen, had he stumbled into a different world? Or had everything he'd seen after he'd lost his right arm and gotten caught in that explosion been a long, long dream? Was his real self still buried under the rubble, on the brink of death?

His delusions nearly trapped him, but he almost wished he was hallucinating all of this. *What if this is a dream a much younger me is seeing…? Would I get the chance to do everything over?*

Nader remembered the promise he'd exchanged with his childhood friend, and the next thing he knew, he was crying as he ran.

I don't know.

Hey, c'mon, somebody tell me.

How do you get to be a hero?

How can a guy like me…become one of those?

He had no idea that at this very moment, Chané Laforet was steeling herself for a fight with him. Unable to be the hero he'd promised to become, he kept wandering through the streets.

Inside the bundle he'd made of his jacket, he'd acquired a bare hint of strength in the form of a small fortune.

He didn't know how to use that strength.

The one and only thing he could do was keep wandering.

⟺

Somewhere in New York

"Look, Miria! Airplanes!"

"Yes, it's Charles! Augustus! Lindbergh!"

On their way to a certain job that Molsa had found for them, Isaac and Miria spotted the seaplanes, which were just pulling out of New York.

After flying very low through the canyons between the buildings, the planes' silhouettes vanished over the horizon of the starry sky. The afternoon's thin cloud cover had cleared long ago, and it seemed to be blessing the planes as they climbed.

That romantic sight plunged Isaac and Miria into excited conversation.

"By the way, we've pulled a train robbery, but we've never robbed a plane, have we? We've turned over a new leaf, so I'm not planning to try it, but still."

"Say, Isaac, what do you do during a plane robbery?"

"Well, you know. You steal what's important to planes."

"What's important to them?"

Isaac mulled over that basic question for a little while. "...The sky?"

It was an extremely straightforward answer.

"Ohhh, you're right! If there was no sky, they'd be in big trouble!"

"Right... Meaning we'd erase the sky from the world!"

"How spectacular! But, Isaac, where does the sky start, and where does it end?"

Isaac answered this second fundamental question with no hesitation at all. "Well, it's wherever a plane can fly."

"But those airplanes were flying reeeeally low."

"...How can this be...? You mean we're already in the sky?! Then, since airplanes fly so low here, couldn't you say New York is a city in the air?!"

"Yes, Machu Picchu! Balnibarbi's Laputa! The Dragon Palace!"

Miria was excited, and neither she nor Isaac noticed that half her examples were wrong.

"I see... We've got a really clear sense of the sky now, thanks to the airplanes. The brothers Wright were truly incredible... Okay, Miria, let's be grateful to the airplanes! We can't steal from them! I'm glad we've turned over a new leaf! What a fantastic feeling!"

"Yes, we're on top of the world!"

With a conversation more suited to children than adults, the pair took off running through the dark clouds that enveloped New York.

They hadn't realized they'd been pulled into a chaotic vortex, and they probably never would.

After all, to them, all of life was a new discovery. It was chaos itself, and it brimmed over with darkness and light simultaneously.

Regardless of whether they realized it or not, as the planes' crazy ruckus subsided, a mantle of deep darkness was falling over the city of New York.

⇔

Late at night In the darkness

In a villa managed by the Runorata Family, Melvi entered a private room that faced the courtyard. He turned off all the lights and lay down on the bed.

Felix, his bodyguard, only accompanied him when he left the villa. There were several dozen mafiosi in the mansion, and right now, a guard protected him.

Somehow, a voice spoke to him.

"Hello there. You were very ostentatious today, Melvi."

It came from a corner of the pitch-black room.

Melvi could hear the curtains swaying. Clearly, someone had slipped past the guards and infiltrated the villa. However, without getting the least bit flustered, Melvi answered the darkness.

"It was nothing important, *my master.*"

"I see, I see. Still, your guard this afternoon was impressive. I genuinely had no opportunity to get close to you."

"Yes, his abilities surprised me as well."

The darkness responded with a muffled chuckle, then informed Melvi of a certain fact: *"My own plans should be in motion soon. They may end up clashing with what you're doing. If that happens, well, I would appreciate if you didn't resent me for it."*

"But of course. You are the master here. I merely do what you say. If you tell me to die, I'll obediently present my head to an immortal's right hand." He was still lying on the bed; only his words were courteous.

"...Not 'gladly,' but 'obediently.' How very like you. It's marvelous. Well, what I want is for you to make use of your position, do as you please, and disrupt the situation."

"......"

"Also, as I'm constantly telling you, I don't like being addressed as 'master.' It's so stiff."

The darkness gave a stifled laugh, then continued, amused.

"You know my name. Give me a nickname or abbreviate it; you may call me whatever you like. Isn't that what I said?"

"...In that case, I shall call you master."

"Ha-ha! Intractable fellow!"

Then silence fell.

After its quiet burst of laughter, the darkness didn't say another word. From the fact that Melvi couldn't hear the curtain stirring anymore, the presence had probably left the room.

Once he was sure of that, Melvi erased the smile he'd plastered across his face all day—and fell into a deep sleep.

He had to rest his heart to prepare for the artificial smile he'd hide behind tomorrow.

⇔

New York Fred's clinic

After so much running after the airplanes and waving, Isaac and Miria had gotten lost. By the time they reached the site of the job Molsa had found for them, it was past midnight.

"Say, Isaac? This sign says they're not seeing patients today."

"Um, Molsa said it was okay if we just went on in."

Even though it was the middle of the night, there were lights on in the clinic. As the two of them wandered around in front of the door, not sure what to do, a young man poked his head out. "Oh. Are you the ones the owner of Alveare said he was sending to help out? They called ahead and filled us in, but you're real late. Uh... Y'know, I think I've seen you two before, somewhere... Well, whatever."

After examining the pair for a little while, he gave a little sigh and went on. "I'm Who. It may be a job, but we're not gonna make you do any doctor-type stuff, so don't worry about that."

At that point, Who broke off and called to a figure that had appeared behind Isaac and Miria. "Hey. Perfect timing, fella. Where'd you go? Oh, here, I'll introduce you. These are the two who are going to be helping us out."

Responding to Who's words, Isaac and Miria turned around and greeted the newcomer.

"I'm Isaac! I'm looking forward to working with you!"

"I'm Miria. It's a pleasure!"

The pair introduced themselves without any hesitation, and the man gave them a soft smile. "That's very kind of you. Thank you. Fred here is taking care of me. My name is Le... Le......"

The man faltered, then went very still.

It was almost as if his mouth had moved against his will.

His face went blank for a moment. *Then, beneath the thick fringe of hair that covered his eyes, the man smiled* and gave his name again. "Beg pardon. My name is Lebreau Fermet Viralesque. The pleasure's mine."

"...Huh? Was that what your name was?" Who looked perplexed.

"Yes," the man said confidently. "It is the one I gave you earlier."

Hiding his darkness behind a false smile, the man began to incorporate this abrupt pair of immortals into his plan.

Little did he know that, for better or worse, his choice would end up drastically changing the course of destiny.

⇔

On that day, a variety of people were pulled into the seething chaos.

They were all under the same sky, and in that sense, they certainly were standing on the same stage.

People gathered, and as they did, fate boiled down and thickened.

Ultimately, who would be the one to steal the pure fragments this distillation produced?

Who, among the countless gathered cards, would become the joker to whom?

No one knew yet. Not the city of New York. Not even the demon himself.

As each individual clutched their chips in their hands, the curtain was about to quietly rise on the hour of the gamble—and all the churning desires that came with it.

AFTERWORD

It's been quite a while. This is Narita.

So, the *Baccano!* series is approaching its tenth anniversary, and the only parts left to tell are this one, *1935*, and the epilogue of the whole series, *2003*.

As the people who've read this volume are probably aware, this arc is going to revolve around both Firo and *him*. Compared to Ladd, Christopher, and the rest of that crew, he's a total nobody. What is he going to do next?

On top of that, one of the strongest characters in the series, a guy who's right up there with Ronny, has completely switched sides. Will Firo, Ladd, and company have a shot at winning?

Not only that, but why does that one guy—who should be a character new to this volume—look so much like that other character?

Will the Croquis clan I wrote about somewhere, at some point, actually appear?

When will Chi and Adele come into it?

Will Dallas and Eve show up at all?

At the beginning of this 1935 arc, there are still a whole lot of mysteries left, and since over half of the existing cast is going to appear in it, it may run a little long.

At this point in time, I haven't nailed down the conclusion yet. Where will the crazy ruckus of 1935 end up? I hope you'll watch it unfold from the edge of your seat!

The childhood friend, the young girl who appears in that one guy's memory, has actually already appeared in a bonus novel for the *Baccano!* anime DVDs. That bonus novel may be turned into a book, like *1932 Summer*… Or it may not. Right now, no one's sure, but I hope those of you who don't know her yet will look forward to finding out what sort of character she is!

Regarding my future plans—to be honest, they're a confused jumble of all sorts of things. Sometimes even I don't know what I'll be writing next, but I'd like to bring *Baccano!* and *DRRR!!* to a stopping point first, then work on *Vamp!*, *5656 (2)*, and *Hariyama, the Center of the World*, while also starting on new stories.

I've been doing more jobs with other companies recently: I got to write a *BLEACH* novelization, I wrote *Danganronpa IF*, the bonus mode for *Super Danganronpa 2*, and I've participated in *Red Dragon* as a game player. As you'd figure, though, Dengeki Bunko's *Baccano!* is where it all began for me, and I'll work hard so you can enjoy the last few volumes, all the way to the end!

Please stick with me until then!

...And now that I've reaffirmed my resolution, I'm sitting here playing *Super Danganronpa 2* and *Dragon Quest X* because the air conditioner's broken and it's so hot I can't work.

So far, in a move to save energy, I've managed to get through it with electric fans and bamboo shades, but what with the exhaust heat from the computer on top of everything else, I'm just about at my limit. And actually, because of this heat, my computer overheats and shuts down even before I do.

I've been cleaning my place so I can call the repair guy, and I keep turning up all these memories I'd love to consign to oblivion, like all the various characters I made. Examples include superpowered characters, *Evangelion* fan characters, and all-powerful pirates. I went to the trouble of printing these things out on a printer. I don't even know how many times I've almost died in agony while I'm cleaning...! I even saw my clumsy attempts at illustrations in there. I don't know whether these tears are from the dust I'm kicking up as I work or the urge to murder myself.

Even so, when I think that all this mortifying history is why I'm here today, as embarrassing as it is, it's still a precious memory and the foundation of all my work, so I think I'll put it away carefully. As far back in the closet as possible. In a cardboard box sealed with a ton of packing tape.

(Mutter...) Besides, to be completely honest, Nebula, which appears in most of my series, and several of the vampires are straight from those mortifying lists of super strong and huge corporations I dreamed up, and my own all-powerful vampires filled up notebooks anyway, *cough*, ahem.

I get the feeling I may have mentioned something that should never be said, but even though the stress and summer heat fatigue are demolishing my gastrointestinal system, I'm feeling great. I've got more energy than I've ever had before!

And that's a lie.

However, I'd like to hurry and get this place cleaned, blow off stress by gaming, conquer the hot summer blahs, and bring you stories in peak condition! Wish me luck!

Oh, and about *DRRR!!*— Incredibly, both the latest manga volume and this book will hit the shelves on September 10th! Satorigi and Kuma, seriously, thank you so much! I'll work hard to ensure that *DRRR!!* and *Baccano!* will each make the other more of a blast!

*The usual thank-yous begin here.

To my supervising editor, Wada (Papio), and the rest of the Dengeki Bunko editorial department. To the copy editors, for whom I always cause trouble by working too slowly, every single time. To the staff in all the departments at ASCII Media Works.

To the people who are constantly taking care of me: my family and friends, and other writers and illustrators.

To Director Omori, Ginyuu Shijin, and everyone else I'm indebted to in anime, manga, games, and other areas of the media mix.

To Katsumi Enami, who's as busy as ever but still drew the terrific characters that grace this last section of the 1930s arc.

And to everyone who read this book.

All the people mentioned above have my deepest gratitude. Thank you very much!

August 2012, Ryohgo Narita